EVERYBODY NEEDS SOMETHING

stories

MELANIE PAPPADIS FARANELLO

This book is a work of fiction. Names, characters, businesses, organizations, places, events, and incidents either are the product of the author's imagination or are used fictiously. Any resemblance to actual persons, living or dead, events, or locales is entirely coincidental.

Some of the stories in this book have appeared in different form in the following publications: "Flotsam" in Swamp Pink, "My Father, My King" in Vestal Review, "Airways" in Connotation Press, "Just Fine" in Adelaide Literary Magazine Best of Anthology, "Arboretum" in Story South, "Everybody Needs Something" in Adelaide Literary Magazine, "Marionette" in Blackbird, "The Auditorium" (at "At the Auditorium") in Fifth Wednesday Journal.

Printed in the United States of America
26 27 28 29 30 p 5 4 3 2 1

EU Authorized Representative
Easy Access System Europe—Mustamäe tee 50, 10621 Tallinn, Estonia,
gpsr.requests@easproject.com

Library of Congress Control Number: 2025943693

ISBN 9798991456531 (paperback)
ISBN 9798991456555 (epub)
ISBN 9798991456548 (PDF)

Published by Columbus State University Press

Marketing and distribution by UGA Press

Cover designed by Peter Selgin

Author photo by Sara Huber

to my family

Table of Contents

My Father, My King

The last time I saw my father, he told me the bearded lady was worth a penny if I ever got a chance to see the circus. I wondered if he was offering an outing—father-son bonding, if he'd pull a pair of tickets from his pocket—and swoop them from behind my ear, magic. Instead, he reached for the perpetual itch across his fleshy chest sprouting tufts of hair that turned golden with the sun, his Hawaiian shirt unbuttoned to the third hole as usual.

His lazy eye made me wiggle. I tried to find the right angle, hoping it'd catch me in its vision, but it always swam away.

Once he brought me fishing. I threw rocks into the creek while he fell asleep in the chair. When he woke, he cursed the sunburn mark across his arm where I'd propped the pole. The hook dangling from its wire, inches above his chin, so if he lifted and opened, I could reel him in.

When my teacher asks the class to write a poem describing our families, I squirm like a minnow beneath that creek's murky water. The other kids, they write about their parents like they're superheroes. They have names like Momma and Daddy, Grammy and Pops. They help so many people—they give stitches in the hospital, fix the streets, answer phones, drive trucks to Iowa, get people out of jail; they clean and cook and carry my classmates on their shoulders, on their backs, bring them to so many places, like the zoo, the circus. Their faces take up half the page, and the teacher says remember to leave room for the writing. I want one of these super-heroes for myself.

In my poem, my father wears a crown, a velvet purple cloak; he is king of a small faraway village where we live in the highest altitude looking down from our peak onto all the tiny people and never get out of breath. My mother is beautiful and still alive. I, of course, catch golden fish every day and buy plump fresh fruit from the market where the bearded lady greets me with open arms and a hug that smells like bread. My teacher praises my poem, compliments the details, suggests I add more metaphors, something to bring it to life.

When my father died, I told my son his grandfather's real name was Frederick, but everyone called him Ralph. My son waist-high beside me at my father's grave, my hand light upon his head, he thought this was funny and he laughed. And that felt like something. Like I'd won a prize at a carnival, some oversized inflatable I'd carry with me the rest of the day, set on my shoulders so it could look down from above, light enough to blow away, large enough to look like something grand, like I'd won it all. Like I'd always had it all.

Flotsam

Three months after Jack's wife died, an old high school flame, Maryanne, found him on Facebook. She'd heard about his wife's death through a long and convoluted grapevine of classmates neither of them talked to anymore. She sent him a private message, offering her sympathy and a road trip to come see her in Missouri to take a dip in her condo's healing pool. She lived in a complex in a small town in the southwest corner of the state, about a 4-hour drive from where Jack lived in Southern Illinois.

"Nearby Cherokee Country," she wrote. "Everyone's got a healing pool. Works wonders."

The pool, she explained when he wrote back, was why she'd bought the place. It was after her divorce from a man she referred to in all caps as THE IDIOT. Never thought to ask what was in the water, but she swore it helped take the edge off.

The thought of a long stretch of road blinding him for four hours, give or take, sounded right. Lately, driving to his construction sites for work, he never wanted to stop. He wanted to keep going, heavy on the gas pedal, make the wheat blur. He asked Maryanne for her address, jotted it down on the back of a napkin leftover from Dunkin's, and told the guys he'd be off for a couple of days. They didn't ask why. They'd known Joan.

Jack was an efficient man even in sleep, taking his 5-6 hours like a pill every night, up at dawn with just enough rest to make him steady as he drank his cup of coffee at the stove. He worked construction outside of Springfield, managing the sites. When he and Joan married and found out about his sperm, they wore down two mutts in lieu of offspring, until the dogs grew old and lopsided.

He always felt he had enough. Commercials on the radio, billboards along stretches of roads to multiple construction sites, fat jets with their skywriting, everyone selling something—he didn't need any of it. He had Joan, the pups, the ranch house he rehabbed himself and the patio, where he and Joan would spend evenings sitting on beach chairs, throwing a hairy tennis ball to the dogs till it got dark.

Then Jack turned fifty-four and Joan turned fifty-two and she got sick.

Still, he went to work, drove past those billboards which seemed even more off the mark as he held the wheel with both hands thinking *how in the hell?* And the dogs slowed down at the same time, the two of them gone, together, just like that. And Jack held his wife in bed, kept his face in her hair, his large calloused hands on her shrinking frame, as they cursed the world. As she worsened, a well of need opened inside of Jack, and then he did want more. More time, more Joan. He wanted everything to just stop moving, slow the fuck down so he could think a minute. Then she died, and he wanted the dogs back, too.

Maryanne's complex was five miles outside the small strip of town which was mostly boarded-up windows along a dusty road. Everything out of business, aside from a generic gas station mini-mart, where he took a piss and bought a pack of peppermint gum. A group of teenagers hung out by a pump, smoking and blasting music from a phone. Jack thought about what sort of trouble a kid could make in a town like this, thought of himself at that age, he and Maryanne making out in the back of his pop's old pickup truck. The kids at the pump let out a burst of laughter, like an insult. So full of themselves, their lives.

He reset his phone's directions and drove past a bowling alley advertising pizza slices and beer, which sounded like a meal right about now.

Maryanne was waiting on a low balcony overlooking the condominium's parking lot. From afar, he recognized her stance, her reddish curly hair, and her curvy figure, heavier than over three decades ago when he knew her in high school, and a memory flashed in his mind of her going down on him outside the closed schoolyard one night when they both had nothing to do. He'd always liked Maryanne.

She whistled the way he used to for his dogs and held up her hand in a wave. He slammed the car door.

When she greeted him with a cheek-to-cheek hug, he didn't recognize her smell, some kind of flowery vanilla. It wasn't bad, just different. She asked if he wanted a glass for his beer, which she'd already opened for him. He declined and took the bottle of Corona to his parched lips, sucking back half with one swallow.

Her apartment was a small, open-floor plan with beige wall-to-wall carpeting. In the bathroom, a can of floral air-freshener. He glanced at a tube of prescription cream but didn't open the medicine cabinet. Her hairbrush was knotted with her long, auburn hair streaked with silvery highlights. He flushed the toilet and splashed water on his face, avoiding the mirror.

"I'd a recognized you in the grocery store," she told him, curled sideways on her white vinyl couch, her knees bare beneath a miniskirt. "You got the lines now." She drew her finger along the side of her face. "Very distinguished." When she laughed, she bore a wide set of teeth that were vaguely familiar. Her curly hair was held up in a clip.

Jack pulled back the rest of the beer, steady on both feet as he stood in the middle of the living room. The whole apartment—kitchen, living room, balcony—blended together. He appreciated the compactness. Each corner had its function.

"You want another?" She nodded at his bottle and got up from the couch. She headed to the curved countertop separating the kitchen.

"How long you lived here," Jack asked, "in Missouri?" following her the few feet to the fridge. A magnet in the shape of an apple stuck to the front.

"Could be anywhere," she said and handed him another bottle of cold beer.

A plastic bowl with cool-ranch-flavored chips sat on the counter. She shook it toward him, offering. Jack arranged himself awkwardly against the counter. He felt like his t-shirt might be on backwards and couldn't get comfortable.

She told him she was sorry when she'd heard about his wife passing.

Jack didn't like the word passing. Joan was dead. Gone. She was there and then she wasn't anywhere. Whenever some loose part rattled in his chest, he'd taken to the habit of rubbing it with the heel of his fist or knuckle of this thumb. First time in his life, he couldn't fix something. He sucked back the beer.

Maryanne's skirt stretched crooked across her thighs. Her bare feet on the tiles, toenails painted a bloody red. She lifted one foot, cracked the tops of her toes against the floor. The air felt like molasses. His thumb found his belt loop and hooked tight, elbow flayed. He took another swig, and the bottle made a suction sound as it pulled from his lips, a little bubble of froth rose to the top, threatening to spillover.

"Gets hot down here," Jack said, by way of conversation.

"Not like Texas. My brother's in Houston. I went down there once, but never again. Came back with a nasty sunburn. All over," she motioned across her chest where the skin was mottled and exposed.

It felt like too much information.

Buckle up, Joan used to say whenever their neighbor Sheila came around and spilled her love troubles to the two of them on the patio while they were with the dogs. Joan had a big soft heart, but she wasn't one to take on other people's stories. He'd always liked that about her.

Buckle up, he heard Joan say now as his old high school flame talked about the sunburn on her chest. Jack knocked at his sternum with his thumb knuckle while she talked.

A snortle came from the corner of the living room. A wrinkled, pig-faced bulldog was sleeping on an oversized pillow. Jack hadn't noticed him before. He nodded at the dog with approval.

Then, Maryanne was right up close, watching Jack's face with interest. In the yearbook, she was Maryanne Molton. In high school, they'd called her Hot Lava. He had no idea if that was still her last name now. Her Facebook profile said Marylinn *Monroe* (the real Marilyn Monroe was taken) because she wanted to keep her privacy. Apparently, she'd had a bad divorce.

She was close enough for him to see a dewy perspiration beading beneath her powdery deodorant marking the edges of her tank top. Her breath, a mix of cigarettes and cool ranch, didn't bother him.

What bothered him about these past three months was how things didn't make sense anymore.

"Hey, heyya," he said, his voice gravel. She took another step closer. He hooked both thumbs on his loops, his feet cemented to the linoleum floor.

And suddenly, her fingers were walking around his T-shirt's collar. She lightly tapped his Adam's apple.

"You ready for a dip?" she asked, her voice covered in gauze. At the soft spot in his neck, her finger paused. She scratched her painted nail through the tufts of hair sprouting upward from his T-shirt.

He took hold of her index finger and wrapped it gently in his calloused hand. She gave him a wry smile. Then she reached behind and squeezed his back pocket where he kept his wallet. He wondered if Maryanne Molton/ Marylinn Monroe was going to rob him. All he wanted was the photo of Joan that he'd folded inside the worn billfold. She could take the rest, his driver's license stating his birthdate, address, and organ donor status. Sure, go ahead. What good were his organs to him if he was a dead man?

Then a nibble at his neck and her tongue was in his ear. It didn't take much. He swung his arm around her backside, and she pressed against him, groin to groin. She knew what to do.

A growl came from somewhere, the snoring bulldog or Maryanne, he wasn't sure, and he didn't care anymore if she was going to rob him or if he was a dead man.

Right there in her white condo, on the beige wall-to-wall carpeting, a rubber somehow in her hands, her painted nails uncurling the second skin around his erection, she squeezed a pop of air from the tip, and crawled on top of him. Heavier than Joan, her auburn hair released from its clip bursting in all directions, as she thrust a few minutes, pinning him to his back, arms spread wide eagle. A little numb from the pressure and the rubber, the carpet chafing his backside, the room spun. Where the hell was he? She bucked and he came inside her.

After, they both lay naked on the living room carpet, staring up at the ceiling fan slowly rotating. She tapped a soft pack of Parliaments against her palm and offered him a cigarette. He accepted one, but didn't light it. He rolled the barrel between his thumb and forefinger while she smoked.

Later, in the bean-shaped pool behind the building's parking lot, she pointed to the field beyond the busy road where two semi-trucks were passing. In the flat distance, two large piles of dirt rose into wide mounds.

"Gus used to call them *the hilltops*" she said, adjusting a strap of her bathing suit. "Like we're in the Rocky Mountains or something. We'd argue about that. It's Missouri, you dumb fuck, I told him."

Jack laughed. He felt more relaxed than a few hours ago when he'd first arrived. His boxer shorts ballooned slightly as he waded up to his hips in the lukewarm pool full of alien green water. It smelled a little sour and bits of debris floated along the surface. The healing pool. It looked like a motel-style, shitty pool that'd never been cleaned or taken care of or treated with any kind of chlorine.

Maryanne was a mermaid, adept in the water, light and flexible, her girth graceful.

"He thought he was a real cowboy."

Jack felt disoriented.

"Your husband?" He corrected himself, "ex."

She laughed without smiling.

He nodded. "Right."

The sky was overcast, but a streak of light broke through the clouds, shining across Maryanne's face. Elbows bent, she glided her hands atop the water, turning slightly left and right in a soft dance with herself. In the glare, she looked almost pixilated. Jack noticed an old man sitting on one of the complex's balconies. Jack wondered what they must've looked like from there. Two middle-aged, out of shape, out of sort, lonely people soaking in a warm piss hole in the ground, waiting for its healing properties to do something.

Maryanne slipped down under the water in one smooth motion, leaving a slow ripple across the murky surface.

Jack squinted out at mounds of dirt, the hilltops, as Gus called them. They would've been friends, he decided, if he and Joan lived here in this complex. He pictured drinking a beer with Gus; Joan and Maryanne sitting by the pool; the dogs howling at the moon which was already visible against the pale sky.

Maryanne resurfaced, her frizzy hair matted to her head.

"I spend a good ten hours a week in here," she said. "My spa treatments." She spit out a stream of dark water. "You'll see. Just wait." She pushed onto her frontside, doing small breast strokes towards him where he remained waist-high.

He could still taste her in his mouth. It was strange, unrecognizable.

"What, you don't swim?"

The sun broke through more and pinched his eyes, casting her in shards. He swayed a little side to side.

"Never took to it," he told her. He'd been with his father, fishing in an old rowboat on a lake. Not more than 6, 7 years old, his father didn't believe in life vests. He rocked the boat wildly as Jack gripped the sides with small fists. The only way to learn, his father told him, is to throw yourself in. That's a life lesson for you, he said, the empty beer cans rolling at his feet. A puddle of water collected in the bottom of the rowboat. And then he was overboard. He remembered his father's grip on the back of his neck, the look of terror behind a hearty laugh as he dragged him back over the side. Jack sat shivering on the cold metal seat the entire way back to shore. Never swam again. He didn't tell this story to Maryanne. Just said, "Almost drowned once. When I was a kid."

She blew a funnel of water through her pursed lips again. It fell in a limp arc. "Who hasn't?"

A surprising laugh erupted from his throat. Tingles on his skin. "Never thought of that before."

She plunged headfirst and swam between his legs, her body pressing against his thighs as she wiggled through.

He wanted to fuck again. He wanted to drive the endless stretch of highway back home. He wanted his old mutts to be waiting for him at his ranch house on the edge of the forest preserve. He wanted to die. He was glad his wife—Joan—would never be in a bean-shaped pool, swimming through some lonely bastard's shaky legs.

Half of a brown leaf was stuck to his wrist. He flicked it away.

Maryanne Molton resurfaced behind him.

He didn't bother toweling off with the rough half-sheets the complex provided stacked on a plastic table. He stood dripping at the pool's edge, pulling on his T-shirt, pushing back his hair.

"What'cha gonna do now?" she asked, her head floating as her body submerged under the water.

Jack shrugged. "Same as always."

"There's nothing much you can do about it. So that's right, I suppose."

"I'm gonna get into my truck. I'm gonna drive home. Wake up."

Maryanne nodded. "Wake up. Every day you wake up."

"Go to work. Go to bed. That's it. And then again."

"That's right."

She kicked her feet out in front of her.

He had a strange feeling of wanting to hug this woman. He didn't know her anymore and yet he didn't know this Jack standing here dripping either. Maybe the pool did something to him.

"You staying in there?"

"Oh, honey, I'm just getting started."

Jacked laughed, a genuine, full laugh that set off a small burst of electricity, warming up the back of his neck, down his arms, inside his chest. Made him think of that powdered Kool-Aid turning the water red. He could still feel the pressure of her swimsuit rubbing through his legs.

"Well then," Jack said. "Thank you for the beer. And the pool. And…you know."

She smiled. Her lip stuck to her front tooth. "You can come back anytime and find me right here. You ever feel like another dip, you come on down."

"Yeah." Jack squinted into the sun breaking fully through the overcast now. "Maybe I will."

"Just head toward the hills."

Jack laughed along with her.

The drive home was dark, and Jack might as well have been driving into space, or some bottomless abyss because he could not feel the truck on the road, everything was smooth, the sky an enormous black ocean in which he was floating. He wondered about that healing pool. About Maryanne. About what Joan would think of him now, but he didn't feel bad. He felt like maybe it was Joan who'd sent him there, to Missouri, to Maryanne… *What a load,* he cut himself off and punched on the radio to snap himself out of it. But the DJ's voice felt wrong, and Jack's skin suddenly hurt, thorns scratching up and down his forearms as the guy talked, and he couldn't even understand what he was saying, and he turned off the radio.

This time he just let himself float into space, into the black ocean outside, and he felt like he was nothing, like maybe he was dead, no longer attached to the Jack on a worksite in Southern Illinois or to the Jack in Missouri standing in Maryanne's pool. His body still existed in both of those places, but without him in it. He was suspended, a collection of molecules, not attached to anything. Nothing but a cluster of ions. Like a ghost. If it wasn't for the annoying nag of his bladder, he would have believed it. But he had to pee.

At the service station, he bought a scratch-off lottery ticket and tucked it into his back pocket. Then he bought a corndog from the metal roller rack. The cashier was a lanky teenager with boiled acne along his jaw. Jack had the unusual urge to talk to him. He wanted to assure the kid the acne would go away one day. It might leave scars, a crater or two, but nothing a little scruff wouldn't hide. On his service station shirt, the kid wore a button that read *Jared.*

Jared handed Jack his change, and Jack took a bite of the corndog, suddenly ravenous. The kid bent over the counter, going back to his phone, and Jack just stood there chewing, watching the kid play his video game. The store was so bright with all its electrical fluorescents.

The kid didn't seem to mind Jack standing there, and Jack appreciated the decency in this. You didn't see that too often anymore these days. He suddenly felt overwhelmed with appreciation for this service station with all its lights. It had everything you would ever need. Bars of soap and every kind of soda and all the snacks and sliced bread and little packets of pain medication and disposable razors and rows of magazines and batteries. Outside was nothing but darkness. The glass windows reflected all the brightness; inside was everything. The corndog wasn't even bad. He could stay here forever. He had nowhere to go.

Through the doors, a couple entered, bickering loudly, interrupting Jack's thoughts. He noticed a large mirror overhead, the kind that is curved and warps everything in its wedge, and in it he saw his shrunken self at the counter.

Enough now, he heard Joan's voice in his head, and he threw out the rest of his corndog. When he stepped outside, everything smelled like diesel, and trash skittered along the ground.

He drove the rest of the way home in silence, no longer floating. The sky no longer a black ocean, the road dipped and cracked as the truck bounced on the uneven asphalt, and as he got closer, he started to feel like Jack again, like Jack in his body, and he had no idea what just happened down there near the border or who in the hell that was wading around in a healing pool, who the hell that was lying sprawled on carpet with his pants around his calves.

He could still smell Maryanne's cigarette, its smoke spiraling upwards in little halos.

A couple weeks later, he found the remnants of the unscratched lottery ticket in the washing machine when he pulled out his blue jeans. The ticket was torn, bits of silvery paper curled into pieces. He scooped the paper from the basin, gathering all the wet, wilted scraps and threw them away. Then dropped his jeans back into the machine to wash them a second time, his knuckle rubbing against his sternum so hard he thought it'd crack.

Outside on the patio, he sat under the nighttime sky, an old tennis ball in hand, the empty recliner beside him. He pitched the ball into the dark. It landed with a quiet thud on the grass. An airy laugh escaped Jack's lips as he pictured Maryanne's bulldog snoring in the corner, his wrinkled mug and hanging jowls steadfast on its pillow in no hurry to go anywhere. It was a good dog. Jack wondered if maybe he had imagined the whole thing—the bulldog, Maryanne, the sex, the pool, the pitch-dark ride home, the kid cashier, the convenience store. It all seemed so far away. Yet part of him felt there was still a Jack eating his corndog inside the bright, bright store, with all its lights that would never turn off, and this Jack would never have to leave, would never have to catch up to where he sat now on the patio, the tennis ball somewhere out there in the dark wet grass. There was still a Jack wading in that strange green pool, too, though that guy was harder to recognize.

He pictured yet another Jack. Thirty years from now, in his hospital room, a nurse quietly adjusting the machinery ticking around him. His eyes shut. Ready to see his wife. Ready for Joan. He put on his finest shirt, a tie miraculously appearing in his hand, and straightened the knot around his pressed collar. Combed over what little was left of his silver hair. It'd been so long. She'd been alone too many years. She and the dogs, too. This Jack waited with shut eyes for his name to be called, to see his wife, to throw a ball to the old dogs too, if there existed that sort of thing. He had no idea. Jack surveyed his organs, the ones he knew by name anyway. *Go on*, he said to each one as though demanding away a stray having wandered onto his property. Stubborn, lost, looking for love. *Go on, go, find a new body to work for, do the one thing you were designed to do, and do it well.*

And then like bits of flotsam drifting across the murky surface of his aging mind, it was Maryanne Molton wading in green water. That singular day, a lost bit of debris having un-wedged itself from his memory thirty years later. How he'd driven through that endless repetition of flatlands and ended up in her dusty Missouri town, how she'd made him laugh, a sputter from an old faucet, and how it was the one thing he had needed. Maybe in another life, he'd come back and thank Maryanne Molton better, thank her for giving him the one thing he really needed and for somehow being the one to know it; he'd come back in another life, and maybe he'd even learn to swim.

He straightened his tie. He could feel his wife. Just over there, beyond the haze. Nothing more than a thin veil separating them. Her loosc nightshirt, her purple sandals, the hairy tennis ball now in her familiar hand. *I'm here,* he called to her. *I'm coming.* Head tossed back, her open mouth releasing curls of relief, smoke signals in the sky. A band sounded in his mind. In the distance, a parade.

Take Me Out

The Latin Ballroom Dance Class was her therapist's idea. Scheduled for Tuesday nights at the local community center, tonight was the first lesson. But if weather was capable of transmitting messages from some higher being, then it was obvious, she shouldn't go. The rain was relentless, turning to sleet despite it being spring.

Leah hadn't taken a dance class since she was a little girl wearing a crooked tutu to after-school ballet. But Latin Ballroom Dance was the only thing on her "Dates with Self" list that Dr. Pasar had encouraged Leah to make. A tangle of knots scratched out her initial three ideas: Order Sushi; watch Hammy drink from his sipper; binge-watch baking competitions. When she'd shown her attempt to Dr. Pasar, her therapist tilted her head like a teacher trying to construct the most diplomatic way to tell a child their work was crap. Apparently, Leah had done the assignment wrong.

"These are all quite...solitary activities," she said, handing back the piece of paper.

"It's a date with myself."

"Yes, but to take yourself out, among other people. Can you think of something that you might enjoy outside of the house?"

Maybe Leah was over-sensitive, a phrase which had always felt unfair, but sure, fine. She discerned a strained patience in Dr. Pasar's tone, and then, a subtle flare of her nostrils from having suppressed a yawn. Not only had Leah failed the homework assignment, but on top of that, she was boring her therapist.

Three months ago, after Nick had left their five-year-long marriage to live on a catamaran, like some kind of made-for-Netflix movie, Leah found Dr. Pasar online and called to schedule an appointment. Nick's reason was he didn't want to turn forty in the suburbs of Connecticut, still working from home in their small ranch house's second bedroom turned office, which was meant, someday, for a baby, which they didn't have, though they hadn't tried.

"A boat?" Leah clarified. He could work from anywhere, so why not? he'd said with an insulting spark of enthusiasm. She knew the *why not* was rhetorical, but she answered anyway.

"Hammy?" she said, quickly realizing how pathetic it sounded. The hamster had been a pandemic purchase, and like the pandemic itself, the pet felt outdated.

It hadn't dawned on her to answer Nick's *why not*? with *us* or *me*, until she recounted the story to Dr. Pasar weeks later.

Dr. Pasar was so poised, expensive horn-rimmed glasses perched on her perfectly sloped nose, touched-up caramel highlights framing her smart face, sophisticated flats peeking out from her hemmed, cosmopolitan pantsuit. Dr. Pasar didn't belong in the suburbs. Leah was glad she had never run into her at Stop 'n Shop or Walgreens. She imagined Dr. Pasar only existing in her office, like how Leah used to think of her elementary school teachers living in their classrooms. Once, in her twenties, when she saw Ms. Ross, her first-grade teacher, in the waiting room at the dentist, Leah still felt strangely betrayed and ducked behind a worn office-copy of *Time Magazine*. She felt like a child seeing the Easter bunny remove his oversized costume-head to reveal an acne-riddled teenager; or Santa in the parking lot getting into his Chevy Cavalier with a cigarette after his post at the shopping mall's North Pole. Leah knew that probably said more about her than the actual situation, but still.

Dr. Pasar didn't take insurance, and Leah spent a third of her paychecks from her web design work to pay for the sessions. The therapist's office was all wooden bookshelves lined with complex hardcovers, an intricate wool rug woven with bloody reds and muddy browns, a leather therapist-armchair coupled with a leather patient-couch. A curved marble coffee table, too narrow to put anything on except a tiny gold clock, which ticked like a metronome counting down the minutes. Leah felt rich by proxy. Urban and classy. At her first session, Leah confessed the office reminded her of a fancy French restaurant, which, to Leah's delight, had made Dr. Pasar toss her head back in a generous laugh, something which had not occurred since.

The dance class started at six thirty p.m. Leah stared at the rain as her kitchen clock creeped toward six o'clock. When pressed to brainstorm about things Leah enjoyed doing with others, Leah had said she liked going out with her friends when they were in college, dancing at bars, but she was too old for that now, and those friends lived on the West Coast. Dr. Pasar suggested the Community Center, which to Leah sounded the same as the Senior Center.

The following week when Leah had brought in the community center's mailer and flipped open to the listing for Latin Ballroom Dancing, she hoped for one of those head-tossed-back laughs again, but instead Dr. Pasar's composed face ignited with approval, which Leah felt warm through her body. "Try it." Dr. Pasar smiled, revealing her perfect teeth. Right there, on the leather couch, with Dr. Pasar observing quietly, Leah pulled out her phone and registered.

It was the sort of thing she would have suggested, partly as a joke, to Nick when they first married, before settling in to scroll the Netflix menu for something to watch together, which they would never end up finding before going to bed. His penchant for historical documentaries, hers for reality shows. Despite Leah pointing out those were just different directions for what was really, when you thought about it, the same genre, Nick was never swayed.

The point was, Dr. Pasar wanted Leah to become her own companion. Her own best friend.

The rain fell, steady and insistent. The sky darkening against the stubborn gray clouds. Leah watched the clock tick past six o'clock. Her hand resting in the bag of tortilla chips, fingers dry with salt. The kitchen fuse kept tripping and needed to be replaced, something Nick usually would have fixed. The raw April chill seeped into her bones, despite wrapping herself in an old flannel Nick had left behind. Any of his leftover warmth having dissolved, the shirt rendered useless. She wore a wool turtleneck sweater, which she usually hated because the sensation of clothing on her neck made her feel claustrophobic, like she was being choked. But today she didn't mind as much. Imagining the light chokehold of someone's hands, she could understand how it might feel almost…erotic. If she'd been into that kind of thing. If she'd been a different person altogether. If, if, if…(Dr. Pasar warned her against this kind of thinking)…maybe her husband wouldn't be stowed away in a boat somewhere, blissfully untethered. The sensation of her turtleneck's grip grew stronger, the house strangling her, the walls closing in. She dusted off her hands, crumpled the bag of tortilla chips and threw it, along with Nick's flannel shirt, into the kitchen trash.

Her baggy blue sweatpants versus the rain; inside versus the chill… she watched Hammy in his cage, considering. It had only cost $30 to register, and she hadn't ordered out, so she could easily justify the loss. "What do you think?" she asked Hammy. The hamster turned away, buried itself under a wad of torn newspapers. In her mind, Dr. Pasar's lips pressed together with disappointment.

Leah stubbornly changed into loose-fitting jeans and a lightweight, zip-up black hoodie, leaving it open a few inches, exposing her clavicle, a part of her body she didn't argue with, a part she hooked her fingers onto whenever she crossed her arms over her chest. Dr. Pasar had pointed it out once. Called it a "protective pose." And then Leah didn't know what to do with her arms or where to put her hands.

The class was in a small windowless room in the basement of the community center, at the end of a long hall flickering with florescent lights. A children's ballet room, with two sets of parallel bars beside the mirrored walls, metal folding chairs lined like crooked teeth. As soon as Leah entered the space, it was 1989, she was ready for her ballet class, leotard and tutu, pigtails. Just as nervous as if she were a child. 1989, her father still alive, her future a crayon drawing; Nick, a stranger.

"Welcome, come on in." The teacher waved. He was a short, white man in his sixties with a yellow fuzzy mullet and plastic glasses. He instantly reminded her of Hammy, if Hammy turned into a person. The teacher's name was Larry, and he wore a bright floral shirt buttoned over a long-sleeve tee, black athletic pants, and brown and white striped bowling-looking shoes.

Leah stood in the corner as the other attendees introduced themselves around the room—a heavyset Russian woman with a crop of white hair wearing a flowy printed top; a petite grandmother visiting from the Philippines with her grown daughter who was quietly translating their introductions while her toddler lay on the floor with a coloring book; and a very tall married couple—the guy looked like a lumberjack, long beard, jolly cheeks, and the woman looked competent, like someone who could clean a dead bird out of a fireplace, barehanded. The couple seemed to exist in their own private bubble where something was very funny between them. Leah tried not to stare. She realized it was something she never had in her marriage. She thought of Nick, but it felt more like remembering a character in a movie or a TV show than a man she had married.

"This is Anthony and Golam," the instructor said, presenting two men who suddenly appeared beside him. Leah had not seen them enter the room. Anthony was stocky with slicked back dark hair and wore a bowling league shirt, and the same dress shoes as Larry's. Golam was thin, his shoulders slightly hunched beneath his white dress shirt, and his gray trousers fitted with a tight belt. They were here to assist.

"Stay awhile," a voice said, startling her. Anthony had somehow crossed the room and now sat in the folding chair beside her. He glanced at her left hand, ringless, as though gathering data. Leah realized she was standing in her protective pose, wrapped tight in her raincoat, rigid like a coat rack.

"Right," she said. "Just a little cold," she justified, returning a smile, which felt weird on her face.

As the instructor continued reading through printed pages of information—local swing dance events, social ballroom nights, cha-cha classes, Leah noticed the tall couple already in their own lock-eyed dance, despite no music playing. Anthony also wore no wedding band. His hand tremored, and he shook it out periodically as though trying to wake it from the pins and needles of sleep. Maybe he didn't want to be here either. She pictured her blue sweatpants still warm on her unmade bed, waiting non-judgmentally for her. But then she thought of Dr. Pasar. One night. She could do it. What was so hard about being by yourself anyway? It's not like anyone entered or exited this world any other way. Everyone was alone. Big deal. She didn't need a date with herself to understand that fact. She'd taken a philosophy class in college. She knew about Sartre and his existential truths. Wasn't the real challenge being with another person? She'd be fine otherwise. It had nothing to do with becoming her own best friend, or whatever. She would explain this to Dr. Pasar at the next session, but first, she'd get through this class, if only to prove her point.

Leah unhinged her fingers from her collarbone, unzipped her coat and draped it over a folding chair.

"Help yourself," the instructor said, standing directly in front of her now, eye level. He held open a cloudy Ziploc bag full of butterscotch candies, Werther's, and individually wrapped mints. His eyes swam behind his plastic glasses. His upper lip twitched a little. Again, Hammy. He shook the bag, offering the candy.

She reached in and took a golden-wrapped butterscotch.

"We'll get started with a basic step," he whispered, conspiratorially, and flashed a generous grin.

Larry explained to the group they would line up facing one another. "Followers on one side, leaders on the other."

Leah calculated the risk of partners, something she hadn't fully considered. Four women, three men, the married couple not included. She moved to the end of the line, arranging herself partnerless.

Followers were the women. Leaders, the men. The year kept creeping backwards, and if it hadn't now felt like 1975, Leah would have been more offended. But somehow the idea of time travel felt comforting tonight. Nobody was waiting for her in 2024.

She slipped the piece of candy into her mouth. Larry pressed play on a portable cassette player. Barry Manilow sounded from its tinny speaker.

Anthony skipped over the elderly woman and positioned himself across from Leah, despite her attempt at averting eye contact. He stepped forward, hands outstretched, open position. The feeling of holding hands was foreign. She couldn't remember the last time she had done so with anybody. She kept her gaze slightly to the right and over his shoulder, her breath locked in a cage.

One, two, three, four—one, two, three, four—one, two, three, four—they marched left right, in place, the merengue, as Barry Manilow sang *Copacabana*.

When it was time to switch partners, she exhaled and tried again for the end of the line.

Larry, Anthony, and Golam were making their way down the row, taking turns leading the women. Leah was instructed to face the mirror and dance with herself while she waited.

She turned to the wall of mirrors, avoiding looking at her face—the face of a soon to be divorced woman, and stepped in rhythm with her reflection. Leah would recount this to Dr. Pasar—literally, a date with herself!—and it would result in one of those head-tossed-back laughs again.

Plastic frames hung crooked on the wall, photographs of young ballet dancers in pink leotards, eyes glinting with innocence, smiles barely containing their protruding grownup teeth. Leah squinted to get a closer look. She recognized her childhood best friend, Jenny Lu, in the picture, and there was Alicia Samson, and Sarah Greenberg…and then there she was, too. There was Leah, smiling from behind the frame in the cluster of leotard girls.

Impossible. Yet, when she looked again, there she was in the photo, her nine-year-old self on the wall.

"Nice eye contact." Larry appeared at her side, talking to her reflection.

The smell of his mint gum brought her back and Leah appreciated it. He'd been teaching this class for thirty-five years, and it seemed like the kind of trick one might pick up along the way. She sucked her candy lozenge and wondered if her breath smelled like butterscotch.

"You're keeping nice eye contact with yourself, that's good," he said, encouragingly at her side.

"I'm actually noticing my escape route," Leah said, pointing to the open door which led to the hallway, half-joking.

"Oh, you're not leaving," Larry said, matching her steps back and forth in the mirror. It was a strange feeling, being trapped by someone who wanted her to stay.

"Golam, come," Larry commanded, and the thin man held out his hands, turning Leah gently away from the mirror, away from the photos on the wall, away from herself. More hands, more contact. Her hand on his shoulder, his hand on her back. He smelled like chicken soup and reminded Leah of a grandfather, her mother's father, from Poland, whom she'd never met.

She rolled the butterscotch candy in her mouth, the sticky disc clacking against her teeth, the artificial flavor of childhood coating her tongue. Her father had always kept these candies in his pockets, saved them from the drive-thru bank, the teller's canister shooting through an electronic portal, like magic. Leah hadn't thought about that in decades. She had been twelve when her father died, though he had already left home by then, two years prior, after the divorce. Still, Leah visited him on weekends. Still, his little girl. When he died, Leah sat in the front row at the funeral service while her mother sat in the back. As his second younger wife read some garbage poem at the podium and cried, Leah glared lasers, trying to burn holes through her ugly face, trying to set the witch on fire.

A sharp pain suddenly stabbed Leah in her sternum. She lost her counting. She was off step. She apologized to Golam who didn't seem to notice. She tucked the candy into her cheek and took a deep breath. She rarely missed her father anymore. But she missed him deeply now as the butterscotch began to dissolve.

Larry shut off the music, and the partners stepped apart.

The clock on the wall read 2:30. Broken. She had no idea how much time had passed.

Larry moved to the center of the room to demonstrate. Everyone watched except the lumberjack couple, who kept dancing, spaghetti-armed, in their bubble. Larry took the grandmother in his arms. Closed position.

They were to make a frame, the instructor explained. The daughter translated. "It's a push pull." He pressed the woman's hand against the front of his shoulder and swooped his hand under her elbow, pulling her shoulder blade close. "There must be pressure, so the frame doesn't fall apart."

Leah pictured the frame of her house collapsing as Nick floated away on his boat. What had happened between them? Lots of people turned forty and lived in the suburbs, worked from home, and stayed married. What had gone wrong?

When it was time for partners, Leah found the corner of the room again. More photos on the wall, and she saw herself again, in her pink leotard, at all different ages. There she was at five, squeezed in the front row between the other little girls. And there she must be seven, a missing front tooth, standing at the end of the second row. And there, a gangly teen, a new growth spurt, middle of the last row, maybe thirteen, though she had already stopped dancing by then.

She washed her hands over her face. She refocused and held up her arms in the mirror—closed position, moving forward and back in the reflection.

"Strong frames everyone," Larry called out, and she tightened her core, stood upright, arms holding the air.

Then, in the mirror, she saw her father.

He was sitting behind her, across the room on a folding chair, the ones arranged for parents to watch. His hands poised for applause, regardless of how she stumbled.

A warm zing washed over the back of her neck. She stopped abruptly, the room spinning as she whipped around.

Her father appeared in front of her. He pulled her near and palmed her shoulder blade with one hand, lifted her fingers with the other. He felt warm, familiar. He led her expertly into the center of the room, one, two, three, four.

"Dad?"

"Hi, LeLe," he said, and at the sound of that ancient nickname, her knees softened. He held her. She tried to match his steps.

"Strong arms," Larry instructed, sweeping by.

Her father smiled, his eyes twinkling. The everlasting candy weighed heavy on Leah's tongue. He leaned his cheek close beside hers and whispered, "Nine times out of ten, the Cubs will strike out. But this might be my lucky year."

Leah let out a breathy confused sound. Of all the things she wanted to ask. "How do you know this dance?" she said.

"One, two, three, four," Larry counted, stepping with the Russian lady across the floor.

Her father moved her gracefully, leading her this way and that, like a professional.

Leah no longer felt her feet on the ground.

And then, just like that, he was gone, and Leah was standing alone in the middle of the room.

Golam held out his hands to her.

She frantically looked back at the mirror. But Golam stepped forward, and took position, securely framing her with his hold.

Her heart was spastic, pounding in the base of her neck, her eyes darting around the space. A wicked-looking doll dangled from the ceiling on a miniature trapeze. It hung above the lumberjack couple like a mistletoe.

Golam danced off beat to what seemed to be a waltz now. Larry swung himself across the floor, waltzing with himself, calling out one on the downbeat, then two, three, instructing them to float on the two, three. The music grew faster, too fast, and Golam's thin neck stretched, making his head wobble, the look of surprise and good-naturedness like a jack-in-the-box, its puppet having popped up in the wrong decade. She wondered if Golam had known her grandfather. The music grew faster, and Leah stepped on Golam's foot, and she said she was sorry. He answered in Polish, then laughed, which made his long earlobes wiggle, and something about it made Leah want to cry.

Golam kept dancing with her, though the music had changed to a country song, and they were in synch now with their steps, and she remembered being a little girl at her cousin's wedding, the only time she had ever danced with her father. How he had led her across the crowded dance floor and how she had felt like a real ballerina when he twirled her under his arm.

At her own wedding, decades later, Nick had offered up his younger brother for the father-daughter dance. The brother reeked like pot, his blood-shot eyes fastened to her cleavage, hands slipping too low on her waist like a boy at a sixth-grade school dance until the band changed tunes, and he slunk away. She had missed her father then, as much as she suddenly missed him now.

A rush of heat flooded her face, tears threatened to burst forth. She willed herself not to cry, not here, not now, and shoved the feeling down, but it was insistent. Leah caught the strange doll's eyes, hoping it would quelch her tears. Someone softly bumped into her, and she turned to see the elderly woman, her face flushed beneath her white hair as Golam palmed her back.

Thankfully, the music stopped.

The group moved back into parallel lines to learn a combination.

Leah hurried to her spot in the mirror, a wild scrambling in her chest. She looked for her father. She wanted to see him again. This time, she looked directly at her face, into her searching damp eyes. She fastened her gaze, lifted her arms, ready for closed position. She sucked the candy, which was somehow still intact, and closed her eyes. When she opened them, her father appeared facing her in the reflection. He lifted his arms to mirror hers, and everything rained inside her with relief.

This time, he wore a suit and tie. Ready for her wedding, or perhaps, his funeral.

"Hiya, LeLe."

She stepped closer to the mirror. Touched her hands to the glass.

"Sammy Sosa hit a homerun. Bases loaded. Top of the ninth. Atta boy, I told him." His laugh warmed a circle of fog on the mirror, at Leah's forehead.

She was about to say something when she felt a tap on her shoulder. She whipped around. Anthony. She shook her head, but before she could turn back to the mirror, he took her in his arms, trapped her in his dance, spinning her this way and that. She tried to break away, his motion made her seasick, she thought she was going to throw-up, and he spun her, and when she turned around, it was Nick, and she was in his grip, his face beating red, and the creepy doll swung faster from its trapeze, and the music was all wrong, and he turned her inside, outside, back and forth, and she pulled apart, and when she whirled back, her father appeared again and took her into position.

"Easy does it," he said and held her slow and steady. She tried to balance herself. Took a breath. Her father rocked her, left, right, as they glided into the center of the room.

"How are you here?" she whispered into his shoulder.

He pulled a plaid handkerchief from his suitcoat's pocket. Then tucked it back and tried again. He reached deeper and pulled out a little plastic frog, a dime-store toy.

"The old man's rusty," he chuckled.

"Dad, what did I do wrong?"

Anthony, in her periphery, was moving closer. She panicked. No, no, no, please, no more. She folded her fingers over the ledge of her father's hand, as he lifted her arm and led her to the other side of the room.

"I miss you, Dad," she whispered. "I've always missed you."

"It was a rainout of a game, but the Cubbies pulled through, nick of time."

"Dad," she tried again, increasing the pressure against his frame, trying for the push-pull. Trying to feel the solidness of arm beneath his suitcoat.

"Why'd you leave?" she said, her voice small, the words slipping out soundlessly.

He opened his mouth, lips pursed, head tilted back and started to sing. A deep belting sound came from the hollow of his throat. Harry Caray's middle of the seventh. *Take Me Out to the Ballgame...*

There was always this song. *Take me out to the ball game, take me out with the crowd...*he bellowed. She heard the rest in her mind as his voice filled her ears. He sang and sang.

Somehow it felt like the answer to everything. Because there was no answer. Because he was already gone. Because he had not left her. Because someone leaving was just another form of what she'd learned in that philosophy class. Really, what was the difference?

An ancient burning extinguished inside her, and a cool relief released her from its hold. She stepped back. Let go. Felt the space expand around her.

Then from his suit pocket, her father pulled a single wrapped butterscotch candy and held it out like a prize.

The music stopped.

Her father was gone.

The lumberjack couple was doing some kind of off-beat jig, no longer in synch. The grandmother and daughter were resting in the uneven chairs against the wall as the toddler slept across their laps.

She glanced in the mirror, but she knew she would not see her father again. The candy on her tongue had dissolved.

Golam's eyes twinkled at her from the end of the line. Anthony was no longer in the room.

Larry rubbed his twitchy nose with the back of his hand, then took her briefly one last time into closed position, and she felt her posture align before she released, and he moved down the line, and she stepped to the beat alone, stronger, nimble. Capable.

Everything would be up to her now, tasks she might have otherwise relied on Nick to do. She could do them by herself, *with* herself. She could replace the kitchen fuse, paint the bedroom any color at all, maybe even clear a dead bird from the chimney, if she had to.

She twirled in the mirror, her father's voice crooning…*buy me some peanuts and Cracker Jack, I don't care if I never get back, let me root root root for the home team…*her reflection steadfast, secure, following her lead.

The Treehouse

"Think we're done with the cold?" Martin asked, as if now, after twenty years of marriage and Jasmine being gone, they could somehow simply talk about the weather. Of course, they were still two people, a husband and wife who woke up each day (miraculously to Dawn, they managed to wake up each day), who fed the dogs (agile despite their old age) and let them run into the unfenced acres behind the farmhouse. Still, they boiled coffee on the stove as the molasses-like quiet filled the space; Martin in his house slippers, folding the morning newspaper, Dawn knitting by the sliding doors that opened to the woods. Still, they managed to do all this despite Jasmine, their seventeen-year-old daughter having gone missing six months ago.

They were still Martin, still Dawn. The dogs, still the dogs. The coffee, the knitting, the mornings. Some things never change. But they were not Martin-and-Dawn anymore. The calamity having taken up residence in that seemingly benign conjunction between their names.

Trudging now after the dogs as the sun burned off the dew, the wet leaves sodden on the earth, their walking shoes sinking into the forgiving mud, when Martin asked rhetorically about the weather—if Dawn thought they were done with the cold. She didn't answer.

She felt the chill in her bones, her body tirelessly refusing her parka's warmth, as she steadied her gaze toward the treehouse still unseen in the distance.

When Jasmine first disappeared, their rural Missouri town went full throttle—search parties, special patrols, amber alerts throughout the month of October. Their seventeen-year-old daughter's face plastered on the high school's social media, the local news, the signs the local church group had made that still clung to every electrical pole from their rural parts into the small strip of town. In storefronts, too. The gas station, the country diner, the bowling alley. The Five and Dime. The Krogers. It wasn't the first missing person in their town. The high school had had their share of troubles. Nobody talked about their daughter the way they did some of the other kids who'd left school early, like the Miller's boy or the Johnston twins. Of course there were rumors, speculations. People needed something to believe, after all—the scaffolding of a story to uphold the unknown. Wasn't that the whole point of Baxter's Bible club, which Dawn refused to join despite the handwritten notes and casseroles left at her door? She and Martin didn't subscribe to any of it. Especially when the gossip sounded like one of the episodes on *Dateline*, a show they no longer found bearable to watch, if they watched anything at all.

The walk to the treehouse this morning felt harder than usual. Soaked leaves lay like dead soldiers, unburied after winter's slow defrost. As they plodded ahead, the earth gave way beneath their shoes, the soft mud pressing into their soles. Morning dew covered the earth, and the trees wore a thin layer of frost that would soon dissolve as the day stretched on.

It was the same walk, yet everything felt different this morning.

Every morning for the past six months, they had walked this quarter mile into the woods. Martin built the treehouse for Jasmine when she was a little girl. A tomboy until she hit puberty. And even then, Jasmine had loved the treehouse, albeit for different reasons. The first time they checked the treehouse, Martin cleared out a few empty cans of Bud Light and a glass jar filled with cigarette butts, neither of which had surprised them. After that, it was only the squirrels nesting in the corner.

Dawn didn't know what they expected, really. But she knew they depended on the quarter mile of woods, a daily stretch of hope, the wooden fort suspended in the maple's wide branches like a beacon, their missing daughter inside, just waiting for the right time to come down, or so they imagined.

Dawn wasn't sure they could ever stop walking to the treehouse.

The dogs were far ahead, out of sight; they knew their way through these woods. Sometimes, one would run back with something gripped between its jaw, and Dawn's heart would hitch, bracing itself for a piece of clothing, or one of Jasmine's bandanas she wore in her hair, or the strap from her army green crossbody purse she carried each day to school. But it was only ever a chipmunk flopping mercilessly between its teeth as the dumb dog drooled, dropping the dead animal proudly at Dawn's feet.

Everything about this walk felt wrong now. The quarter mile stretch, impossibly long. Dawn struggled to open her lungs, pursing her lips to sip in the air. The cold scratched her throat raw.

"Seems like we might be turning a corner," Martin said, answering his own question about the weather.

A puff escaped Dawn's nostrils, silent and airy. Martin knew she didn't like talking about weather. It was like painting a picture of air—just air, she once tried to explain.

By December, despite Dawn and Martin's objections, the police had called off the search—a fact the young officer reminded them of last night when they returned to the station with Suzy, hopeful at the chance to reopen the case. But by the time they returned home, they were in a stalemate. Neighbors a mile down the road had long stopped dropping off tinfoil wrapped meals; daylight shortened, and one long continuous night seemed to stitch together the winter months. Christmas came, an empty living room, the sliding glass door reflecting Martin and Dawn's shadowy bodies like ghosts, the nightly news on low, reporting on everything but their missing daughter. They seldom left the house, except for their walks to the treehouse or when Martin went to the warehouse, which he'd cut down to twice a week, managing the rest from home. The scarf Dawn was knitting grew into an endless, useless sail.

The ides of March came, and Jasmine turned eighteen, though Dawn had refused to recognize it. To Dawn, it was still October 4th, the last day her daughter had woken up in their house, eaten a sloppy bowl of cereal over the sink, pulled a purple bandana around her auburn hair, slung her camouflaged purse across her body, and walked to catch the school bus that stopped every morning on the corner at 6:52 a.m. The cereal bowl and spoon were still in the drying rack.

The dogs barked in the distance now. Maybe a squirrel, or a deer. They got their share of deer through these woods. Some black bears, too. Dawn worried about the bears. But Martin locked their bins with bungees, and when the honeysuckle bloomed, hung windchimes he'd made from pipe. It managed to keep them mostly away.

Dawn's breath felt ragged. Like a faucet sputtering rusty water from its pipes after not being used. They plodded ahead, not quite beside one another, but slightly askew, Martin in his short-sleeve black T-shirt and down vest—a combination which made absolutely no sense to Dawn given the spring chill. Spring always felt like an insult, sunny skies deceiving, never quite warm enough so why not just keep the parka and hat? Which she did. Gloves, too. Whereas Martin, at the first sign of blue sky, was quick to shed his bulky flannel and canvas coat. He embraced the change of seasons openheartedly, eager as a child, as though spring would suddenly become generous and predictable rather than insidiously erratic, fitful with its sudden outbursts of sleet following a glorious warmth having tricked the perennials into baring their buds too soon.

Jasmine was a bit like this as a child, Dawn thought. Sunny one moment, stormy the next. But weren't all children erratic little fools? She remembered the parent-teacher conferences in elementary school, the way the teachers cloaked their language to mollify adults—using words like *spirited*, rather than disruptive or unruly, suggesting things like *redirection* and *incentive charts*, rather than punishment or reprimand.

Dawn always felt they had gotten it wrong as parents, like a lid that didn't seal quite right. Did they provide enough security and assurance? Dawn could never pinpoint what made her daughter seem unfamiliar to her at times. She imagined having missed some vital page from an instructional booklet that she wished had come with the baby after they left the hospital seventeen years ago. Her own mother would have scoffed at such an idea, having no room for fancy notions like this when one was just trying to get by, but her mother was long gone, and not the kind to lend advice. Nobody told you the important things. The things that really mattered.

"Supposed to get some light showers midday," Martin continued, scanning the sky as he lumbered ahead. A battery running on fumes. "They say it's coming from the east." Her husband walked with a slight limp, one leg slightly shorter than the other, the sort of walk that hinted at some ancient injury or a story to tell. But Martin's limp had been with him since he was a child learning to walk, and Dawn knew him by it as well as she did the timbre of his voice, which bothered her now. What did it matter if they got light showers midday? Or for that matter, what direction it might come from. What was the point of turning on the TV to listen to someone under bright lights talk about the weather when one could just open the window or step outside to feel for themselves what the temperature might be? All of it was nonsense, futile, and here they were in the actual outdoors, Martin insisting on his report. A low rage roiled at the base of her sternum, and still she didn't answer him, because really, what was there to say about any of it? Because if she opened her mouth, she was afraid of what kind of monstrous trapped creature might fly out. Because after everything that had transpired last night, she hadn't slept.

Yesterday, around three in the afternoon, the doorbell rang. Their doorbell never rang. So when Dawn heard it the old panic, which had become shrouded by weariness, sparked and gave a little jolt inside her chest. She opened the door.

Suzy stood hunched apologetically on the front steps. The girl was the same age as their daughter, best friends since kindergarten. But Suzy was smaller framed, bony, which made her appear younger. Her stringy hair hung over her shoulders, frayed jean shorts and an oversized cropped sweatshirt with a faded rock band on the front. She smelled like the cigarettes that Dawn understood the girl smoked.

"Um," the girl said, legs crossing like she had to use the bathroom. "Hi, Mrs. Mathews."

Dawn stared at her.

She held up her phone, a dirty red case with gold flecks, a crack across the bottom of the screen, and waved it limply in the air.

"Suzy?" Martin suddenly appeared at Dawn's side. "Come on in, kiddo." He pushed the door, holding it open, and she ducked past him as she stepped tentatively inside.

The girl's posture wilted as she curled inward, crossing her arm over her bare midsection. She stuck out her phone for them to see.

"It's from Jasmine," she explained.

Dawn grabbed the girl's bony shoulder. Martin yanked on his readers. They huddled close, squinting over the cracked phone in her palm.

And there was Jasmine. A grainy photo, a selfie. Their daughter, riding on the back of someone's motorcycle. On a road they didn't recognize. A rocky wall of boulders rising behind her. Strands of hair whipping from the wind, or from the speed, across her face. Her lips pursed, ready for a kiss.

Dawn felt her knees buckle, her legs give out. Nobody spoke. A wasp nest shook inside her, swarmed with frantic questions, all of which tried to buzz out at once, clogging her throat. "What…when…why… where…who…how?"

She bent over, grabbed her thighs.

Martin's thick fingers were pinching the grease-streaked screen, trying to enlarge the photo, as though he could somehow reach their daughter if he zoomed in close enough.

"Here," Suzy took over, scrolling down or up with an expert flick of her thumb to find a string of messages. It was the first she had heard from Jasmine. The texts had come from a number with an out-of-town area code.

They squinted over the phone, trying to make sense.

Ride or die, she wrote in one text message. *Ya ever go 100 on a harley, better than coke*, she wrote in another. *Off-grid baby,* the caption read beneath the selfie.

The motorcycle belonged to a guy named Rex, who Jasmine had apparently started dating earlier that year. Suzy told them she didn't really know Rex because he was twenty-five. "Or maybe, like, twenty-two?" she said as though it made a difference. They'd met at a party, she didn't remember where, and she said his nickname was T-Rex, or something. He wasn't a bad guy, Suzy tried to reassure them, sitting in their living room after showing them the texts and fielding their questions. Questions that at first sputtered out and then released in a storm of need, a cavernous desperation for answers as they guided her anxiously to the couch.

"They're like, actually really into each other," she told them. "It's kinda gross, but whatever, I mean it's cool though, you know, cause at least she's, like…" Suzy wiped her wrist across her nose, her bare legs bouncing like she was readying to bolt. She seemed to lose her train of thought.

"She's what?" Dawn prompted, wanting, wanting, sitting too close.

"Um…seeing the world?" Suzy shrugged, curling into herself. "Or whatever, I guess?" She pushed up her sweatshirt sleeves, revealing goosebumps rising along her forearms and crossed them tightly around her middle.

They persisted—what party, whose house, where was the guy from, who was his family, had their daughter ridden on his motorcycle before, had she said anything about her plans, where was she...Suzy answering with variations of I'm not sure, I don't really know, um...I think so... until she quickly lost steam and then just stopped talking, her shoulders tight by her ears.

The girl was hesitant at first, but the three of them got into Martin's truck and drove together to the station with Suzy's phone, hopeful, ready to present the first piece of evidence since their daughter had disappeared.

Dawn gripped her cell phone in her pocket now as they walked, still hoping to feel it buzz. But it lay silent as usual against her padded mitten. Suzy's texts were the first they'd heard anything about their daughter since she had been missing. When they tried calling the number, over and over it went straight to a voicemail that had not been set up.

At the station, the officer on duty was a junior cop, the head detective having retired two months ago. A flatness to his face seemed unwilling to emote anything deeper than whatever skimmed across its surface. His eyes were neither cold nor warm, but rather devoid of anything that might tether him to two parents of a missing teen showing him a dirty red and gold flecked phone with cracked screen, as though waiting for some kind of approval. Dawn registered the disconnect. They'd arrived with a decapitated chipmunk in their jaws, ready to drop it at the officer's feet like the damn dogs, their eagerness mismatched to the situation. He did however seem to notice Suzy tucking her stringy hair behind her ear riddled with studs as he drew a measured assessment of her long legs protruding from the frayed jean shorts, her cropped sweatshirt revealing the skin of her belly. Unaware, or maybe accustomed to this kind of gaze, Suzy stood unmoving, staring into the white linoleum floor, like an arctic owl trying to make herself invisible.

An oversized 7-11 cup sat on the officer's desk, sweating beads of moisture beside their daughter's closed file. Martin handed over the selfie that they'd printed at one of the kiosks inside the supermarket on the way. The officer set the photo atop the file and said technically the girl was eighteen, a legal adult, and if anything, all this did was close the case even tighter, for here was proof, she was fine. Dawn was aghast. Before they left the station, Martin tapped the granulated enlargement, pointing out, as though it somehow made a difference, as though it would somehow change something, that their daughter was wearing a helmet. "She's wearing a helmet," he said. A fact nobody could dispute, a fact that otherwise held no meaning.

The treehouse was getting closer, and the thought of it suddenly flooded Dawn with dread. They shouldn't have come. Not today. It mocked them. The trees mocked them, too. The forest, the mud, the squirrels scurrying into their holes. They all knew better. They all knew better than Dawn and Martin.

She noticed Martin rapidly rubbing his thumb and forefingers together, a gesture she knew to be either hunger or stress. When he worried, his fingers sometimes went numb, and he'd rub them like this to regain the feeling. When he wanted a second helping but had already eaten enough, he'd do the same, elbow perched, fingers rubbing, eager like a hawk's talons ready to swoop.

Dawn slowed her pace. Her breath wouldn't come right. She wanted them to stop walking. To keep them from arriving at the treehouse. She wanted to tear the false beacon down, cover their well-worn tracks through the stretch of woods.

She couldn't keep pretending.

Martin was musing about the impending showers.

Dawn's lungs burned. Something fitful thrashed inside her, fire in her blood despite the chill that froze her bones.

Last night at the station, Dawn had emitted the strangest sound, as though some kind of wounded animal was stuck inside her chest, crying to be released. Nobody else seemed to notice. But it startled her, made her feel a stranger in her own body. She couldn't reconcile the relief at seeing the text messages with the renewed anguish. She wanted to ask Martin what they had done wrong? If Jasmine hated them—she must hate them to do such a thing. If they would see their daughter again. If she'd come back. If she'd be ok. If she was going to be ok. If, if, if…a match striking over and over.

A sudden blazing heat ignited inside her. She pulled off her mittens, unzipped her parka. She wanted to reach out and grab the patch of psoriasis crawling across her husband's elbows. She wanted them to stop. Why had they come today?

Yet, this morning when she heard the familiar sound of Martin in the kitchen, boiling coffee on the stove, she was relieved. She would get up. They would walk to the treehouse. She loved her husband in that moment, or rather she loved the consistency of him, like a clock; she loved the familiar tick, steady, carrying on. After coffee, Martin slid open the doors, patting the dogs on their rear ends, sending them off into the unfenced acres and tied up his shoes. And then Dawn pulled on her parka, too, and they started out as though nothing had changed.

"The ground should thaw soon enough though…" Martin said, humming along in conversation with himself or maybe the trees or the air, she didn't know. But he no longer waited for her reply.

She remembered watching a movie on TV once that showed a goat being sacrificed in some rural village somewhere in another country, and how the goat kept baa-ing even after its head was cut off. The head just lying there on the dirt, rolled off to one side, making sounds, not yet understanding, or maybe understanding, that it had been severed from its body. She thought of that now.

They reached the clearing where the path rounded to the right, and they passed the old trees by memory. Martin and Dawn could walk this route with their eyes closed. Another few yards, and the treehouse would be visible. In summer when everything was in full bloom, the structure would be slightly camouflaged by leaves. But this time of year, it was skeletal, sticking right up from within the tree's bare branches.

She forced a cough, focused on sipping in the air. Her chest got tighter.

A few more yards and there it was.

A simple clubhouse. A hideaway. A place to be a child, to make believe, to read magazines, and later to kiss boys, to smoke and drink. A bunker in the sky. Just a quarter mile from homebase. What fools they were to make this pilgrimage today. Their daughter on that motorcycle, hair whipping across her face, pursed lips, in the corner of the photo, a gray shirtsleeve belonging to the prehistoric dinosaur who was riding their daughter away, driving her away down some windy rocky road.

At the trunk, Martin yanked up his pant leg like he usually did before he climbed the ladder while Dawn remained on the ground, watching from below. But now he paused, one hand clutching his pantleg, and a look of uncertainty swept across his face.

"Go on," Dawn said, the words sharp with urgency. They had come this far. Too late to stop now.

Martin said something indecipherable, which sounded like a plea, or maybe Dawn's name, she wasn't sure. He didn't move.

Fine. She'd go up herself. She stepped in front of him, set both her hands on the wooden rung and hauled herself up, one step at a time. She pulled her body into the treehouse, ducking as she stood. Then Martin ascended behind her.

They stood together in the small space. For the first time, they stood in the treehouse together.

Dawn dropped to her knees and began brushing out the remnants of the abandoned squirrel's nest, letting the branches and sticks fall to the ground below. Wide sweeps of her arms and hands, removing debris as dust flew in her face, dirt in her hair. A prowess overcame her. She swept and swept until it was clear. Martin, there or not, behind her.

When she was done, she stood and wiped herself off, then without a word, crawled down the ladder the same way she had come up.

The dogs appeared, waiting, happy and loyal. The sight of them gave Dawn a swell of gratitude. She pulled a stick from her hair.

As they headed back through the woods, a different silence descended.

They stepped over damp logs and matted leaves, unwinding their way through this territory they knew so well, crossing the half mile of land that if one kept going would extend toward route 99, and even further, right into the parking lot of the Kreugers that went up last spring, and beyond that across the Butler's farm, which had been ravaged last summer from the drought, Bob Butler never fully recovering from the toll it took, but word was it also had something to do with little Robbie going off to Afghanistan and coming home six months later only to be shipped off again, and beyond that the Elmwood subdivision where some of the bible folks lived, and even further to some windy road with a wall of boulders where their only daughter was riding away, but that was a place they didn't know and Dawn stopped her thoughts from going there. But this here—that elm, and the fallen oak, and the poison ivy crawling around that rotted stump, and the patch of clover around the bend, they knew this stretch of woods as well as the dogs who'd learned their way since they were pups.

But none of that made Martin's strange reticence any better. His silence unsettled her.

He walked a few feet behind her, hands in his vest pockets, head down as though watching the ground for any hidden explosives. Dawn didn't like it. She didn't know what to do.

She wanted to tell him they still had the dogs, and these woods, and this walk to the treehouse, though maybe they shouldn't come anymore. Maybe today was their last walk through the woods. It felt like a movie set after the crew had gone home, Martin and Dawn wandering in what used to be.

On their way back, Dawn saw their small house rising in the distance. The awning sagged above the back deck. The weeds would have to be taken care of. She'd order some mulch. Things Dawn hadn't considered in months. She would consider them now. She would think about everything she had neglected. It was the two of them. Martin and Dawn. It would have to be enough. What else could they do?

Even Martin's footsteps were too quiet. She felt if she were to turn fully around, he would dissolve in her periphery like a ghost. Her heart skittered. An urgency fueled her.

"It does seem like it," Dawn said, entering the conversation that Martin had started earlier about the weather, about whether they were done with the cold. And to her surprise, the battalion eased inside her.

"I'd say we're in for a warm stretch," she said.

She glanced at her phone, still silent, no messages. She clicked on the weather app. It felt important to be accurate. "Looks like the rain'll hold off till later this afternoon, around two."

Silence and then "Hm." A simple sound of acknowledgment. A bite.

Something eased, smoothed the jagged air between them. She realized it was better than not knowing how to address the mess neither of them understood how to clean up, all sharp edges waiting to pierce and cut and blame, and beneath that something dangerously sodden, a cavernous quicksand that would swallow them whole if they were to step into it.

"Probably reach seventy today, if we're lucky," he answered, finding a new stride. And there was such generosity in it, Dawn felt everything expand.

They emerged from the woods and began walking across the field toward their unassuming house at the edge of the grass.

"I noticed the daylilies pushing up," Dawn said, unsure whether or not she remembered the heads pressing through the mud. It didn't really matter.

"I'll get to making that border soon as the ground softens," Martin responded. "I've got the bricks stacked out by the shed." His voice was comforting now.

They approached their house in synch, walking beside one another.

Dawn thought of something written on one of those brochures the bible club had left with their casserole a couple months ago—the kind of phrase she thought was for support groups for people with addictions. But there it was in her head, fumbling around or sort of floating past.

As Martin regained his rhythm, talking about the bricks and the border he wanted to build around the flowerbeds, she soaked it in. Her lungs opened, the air moving more freely now. There was an endless source they could draw from, these stupid accumulations of the life they'd lived together, the daily mundanities offering a bottomless well of things to get done, to talk about. These things would always be there. She loved the perennials then almost as much as she loved the dogs. Almost as much as she loved the air, but she didn't say so.

As they walked slowly toward the house, the sliding doors ready to welcome them, take them back inside, she said, "Maybe we could re-stain the deck."

Martin nodded, understanding, finally speaking the same language, one they could both understand.

"It's something to think about anyway."

She felt him move closer as the dogs brushed past their legs.

I.

Just Fine

The waitstaff at the Heritage Diner were dressed as Christmas elves despite it being the middle of August. It was the last day of Will's short visit before he would leave Orlando and fly back home to Chicago, and he brought his father here this morning because it was the same place they always came for breakfast whenever Will came to town, and because breakfast was something they understood between them, something they knew how to do. Will also brought his father here this morning to tell him, finally, about Linda. Although, he wasn't quite sure how to say it.

"I'll tell you something," his father said now from behind his newspaper. "You know how to tell a politician is lying?"

There he went. Same as always. Will nodded grandly. "If they're opening their mouth," Will muttered.

"If they're moving their goddamn mouth. That's right. I tell you that before?"

"Let's order." Will looked around. "We need menus."

"You go ahead."

"What do you want?"

"Breakfast."

"That's all they've got, Dad. Breakfast. All day."

"Well, good then."

Maybe he shouldn't even tell him. What would his father say? *Five years—that's all it took to destroy?* Or maybe it'd just be that look—a flash of disappointment, another example of how Will failed—like moving from design into digital marketing. "Robbery," his father had said when Will explained the new job.

"I'll get a menu." Will pushed back from the table.

"Jingle Bells" played over the diner's speakers. A fake Christmas tree decorated with ornaments and tinsel stood haphazardly in the corner, leaning crooked in its base. The front of the restaurant was crammed with people dressed in summer attire waiting for a table.

Set in a parking strip next to a nail salon and an out-of-business carpet store, the diner was the same one they had been coming to over the past five years since Will's mother died. Its windows were decorated with fake snow and colorful blinking lights. The same yellow signs from when Will last visited nearly a year ago hung in the empty carpet store's window, *Store Closing! Everything Must Go!*

Will approached the counter crammed with day-old pastries for sale.

"How many?" the hostess asked. She wore an elf's hat with jingle bells dangling from its tip. Two red circles were drawn on her cheeks as though to make her appear jolly, though to Will she looked tired, in need of a cigarette or a drink. He hadn't had a cigarette in over fifteen years, but he craved one now.

"I just need a menu," he told her.

"Look at the decorations!" a mother exclaimed, wiggling with her two children in front of Will. "What's all this?"

The hostess replied, "Christmas in August."

Will moved over to make room.

"Look kids, it's Christmas!" She tugged her children's sleeves to peek inside the main room.

The hostess shot Will an irritated look, and it reminded him of Linda. His ex-wife. Ex—he wasn't used to that yet.

She slapped a plastic menu onto the counter and Will took it.

His father was staring off somewhere beyond the windows when

Will returned. As long as Will could remember, his father had been gazing away, so far sometimes he seemed to disappear.

"I've got some news," Will said as he sat down.

A waiter dressed in an elf costume arrived at their table and poured them coffee. Will ordered them two combo plates, sunny side over with sausage.

"What time you leaving?" his father asked.

"After breakfast. I'll drop you home and make my way to the airport."

His father shook his head. "I'm going into the salon." He opened his paper napkin and set it carefully over his coffee, trapping the steam. "The girls get busy on Sundays."

"Why?" As far as Will knew, his father only went to the mall these days to walk his lap before the stores opened. He'd stopped working at the hair salon years ago.

"I tell you about that one time? You would've thought…the way she hollered. I showed her the comb right there on the floor. I tell her *there it is* but I'm trying to get up and she's swatting me like some kind of dog. In front of the whole damn business."

Will stared as his father folded back a corner of the napkin, took a drink of his coffee, and covered it up again. He was the only person in the world Will knew who drank coffee this way.

"That happened years ago, Dad."

His father went back to his newspaper, so Will looked for a sports section, but it was a magazine or weather. He picked weather, opened then shut it without bothering. He surveyed the room crowded with families as though they were part of a set, a different world.

It had been some time in the making, but the divorce was just now complete. The funny thing was, he didn't feel the freedom he anticipated. Not so much free as lost. He was thirty-eight. He guessed plenty of guys his age understood things like love and how to keep a marriage going. He'd never really understood anything according to Linda, who'd reminded him of this so many times that he couldn't determine whether it was her voice or his own saying it anymore.

Across the room, a baby screamed. The baby was smacking a spoon against the highchair as the parents worked together stacking jelly containers on his tray. Will wondered what it would've been like if they'd had a child. Linda didn't want children. And just like other less significant things, like wall-to-wall carpeting and electric toothbrushes, he'd somehow acquired her position on babies as well. Five years married and most of it spent in the kind of annoyance one feels when bumping into a stranger, the two of them navigated what felt like a collision of their lives rather than a union.

"The honest truth," his father grumbled.

Will hadn't worn his ring for months, but he was still in the habit of folding down his ring finger and rubbing his thumb over the bare skin where the wedding band used to be. Not that he owed it to his father, but he knew he should tell him. Will's mother would have known right away. But now she was gone, and in her absence, they did not how to manage the space she once occupied.

The elf came over with their plates. "More coffee?"

"What's all this?" his father said accusingly over his eyeglasses.

"Your food," Will answered. "He's fine, no coffee," he said to the waiter.

"Why the hell's he dressed like that?" his father said.

"It's a thing. I don't know. Christmas in August."

His father looked offended. "What the hell are you talking about?"

"Forget it. Let's just eat." He dug his knife into a small pad of butter, unearthed the square from the plastic tub and pressed it onto his toast. "Dad, there's something I want to tell you."

Three box fans propped in the open windows did nothing to relieve the suffocating mugginess. Will took a drink of water. "I've got a new place. It's a studio, more like a loft."

"You know we paid outright for our condo when we moved down here?"

"Yeah, yeah I know."

"Cash." His father nodded. He took a bite of his eggs, his jaw flexing as he chewed with small fast movements. He jerked his gaze upright. "You down? With the finances?"

Will was sweating. "Jesus. I don't need money for fuck's sake."

"Debt's a fool's business. When your mother and I moved to Florida, you know how we bought the condo?"

"You just said that."

"That's all," his father said, the loose skin quivering beneath his chin.

"It's about Linda."

"Huh?"

"For god's sake, Linda. My wife?"

His father waved like he was swatting at a fly.

"We split up. Divorced. It's official now. I thought you should know."

A chorus started up in the back of the diner, a group of waiter elves gathered around a table, singing and clapping, "Happy happy birthday, happy happy birthday from all the elves to you!" A few tables joined in the clapping. Will's father was concentrating on cutting his sausage into pieces.

The baby started to scream again. The parents huddled, undoing the highchair's seatbelt, wiping the plate of strawberries, and picking up the baby almost in unison, until the mother finally took over bouncing and hushing while the father worked on the mess. Will pictured Linda in her business suit holding the infant at arm's length. Or maybe, she would've been different, cradling him tight like the mother was doing now, letting his strawberry hands leave stains on her crisp white blouse.

Somewhere a glass broke. A plate dropped. The register opened and shut. The door dinged. The din of conversation resumed.

He wished his father would stop cutting his goddamn sausage.

"Truth is," Will said, wiping the sweat from his forehead, "she found someone else. I mean, there was Jones. But I guess there were others, too." The familiar rage roiled through Will. "Maybe it was a free ticket. So now we can do this, right?"

He took a napkin to his neck. "Jesus, you'd think they have air conditioning in here, being *summer* and all," Will said, "in Florida."

His father chewed his sausage, his jaw popping.

Will spread open his hands. "That's my news."

His father took his napkin and gave a long hard blow of his nose before wrapping it into a ball and tucking it beneath his plate.

"I tell you Mark's wife passed? Ninety-seven that woman was."

Will's mouth went dry.

"That's a nice long life."

"That's it?" Will said.

"And then he gets shingles," his father continued. "Says it burns like hell."

"Did you even hear what I said?"

His father spread his palm over the top of his newspaper like he was petting a dog.

"Dad?"

"I'm sitting right here in front of you, aren't I?"

Will stared back. "I'm divorced now."

So many years, Will had waited for some alternate father to show up. He felt the foolish weight of his expectation press down on him now.

"It's too bad," his father muttered. He folded back the napkin and took another drink of coffee. "Burns like hell," he said, re-draping. "I saw a sign for shots at the pharmacy. So, I walked over myself after that. Son of a gun."

The fury flooded him with heat. "It's too bad?"

His father didn't respond.

"Just like how the politicians are screwing us over?" Will challenged.

"Same story every day."

Will bit his lips.

"I can read any day here. Won't make a difference."

Will made a cage with his fingertips. "Like the lady who was upset about you crawling around her legs? You didn't have a clean comb?"

He snapped his gaze toward Will. "What in the hell are you saying?"

"I don't know. Should I shut up?"

A woman turned from the next table. He didn't know who to yell at anymore. Linda, his father, himself. Nothing made him feel any better.

"Drink your coffee," his father said.

Will obeyed, but it was already cold.

A loud crash sounded from across the room. The fake Christmas tree had fallen over. People jumped from their seats and children started to cry. Ornaments shattered in silver and gold shards across the floor. A group of elf waiters rushed around the tree. A manager, not dressed in Christmas attire, shouted apologies into the room as the elves lifted and propped up the tree.

Will's father pointed his fork towards the commotion. "What's that they've got over there?"

"A Christmas tree."

His father paused mid-slice, his voice rising, "Why the hell's a Christmas tree in the middle of summer?"

"It's…never mind."

"Jesus," his father shouted, dropping his knife. A line of blood filled his palm, and Will stood from his seat, grabbing a napkin.

"What the hell, Dad?"

"I cut my goddamn thumb, right here with the knife." He dunked a wad of paper napkins into his glass.

"Get off, will you?" He knocked Will away.

"It's getting all over."

Will removed the sopping clump of napkins from his father's grip. "You don't need all these." He folded a single dry napkin carefully around the cut, still bleeding.

"It's the goddamn medicine. They tell me I'm not supposed to cut myself."

He didn't know what medicine his father was on.

"Just squeeze it," Will said.

"I'm gonna need a stitch. You see here," he pointed to his jaw. "A nick shaving, you would've thought I'd killed a pig in my bathroom."

"All right, all right. Let's just go take care of this, okay? Come on." Will took some money from his own wallet and dropped it on the table.

"Get the hell outta here. Put that away," his father shouted.

"Just leave it. I got it. Let's get you somewhere for this cut."

"I'll be damned, you put your funny money back into your goddamn pocket, or I'll stay here bleeding over this goddamn place."

Will could feel the diners watching them. He folded the cash back into his wallet as his father used his good hand to fish in his billfold.

The urgent care clinic was empty aside from the receptionist who told them to sign on the clipboard and have a seat. Will picked up last month's copy of *Sports Illustrated* and waited in a gray upholstered chair after the nurse called in his father. It was quiet, no TV, and he tried to read an article, but the words were a jumble. He checked his phone. Still no messages, no missed calls. It had been months since Linda called. Maybe it was being here, away from all the things to which he had recently attached himself—his studio apartment with hardwood floors, his non-battery operated toothbrush that he bought as though making a point, the new corner deli where he got his daily Italian subs to bring to work, the perpetually late #52 and the driver who whistled the same tune every morning—some mix of half songs Will could never grasp.

When his father returned to the waiting room, he had a bandage neatly wrapped around his thumb and a pale exhaustion on his face.

"You okay?" Will stood, but his father was already walking past.

"Let's get out of here.

"Excuse me." A young doctor appeared in the waiting room and introduced himself. "Are you Mr. Leonard's son?"

"Yes?"

"I was hoping to talk with you before your father left. Do you have a minute?"

"Dad, hold on," Will called. His father was opening the door to leave.

In the examining room, Will sat on the chair against the wall.

"Your father still lives on his own?" Dr. Michaelson said.

Will nodded, conscious of their proximity.

"How would you say he's doing?"

"Fine," Will answered quickly.

The doctor's face was impassive.

"He cut his thumb at breakfast. There was a lot of commotion," Will explained.

The doctor wrote something in the chart.

"I should get him home. I think he's tired."

Dr. Michaelson looked up. "I think it would be a good idea for your father to have an assessment."

Will crossed his ankle over his knee, then uncrossed. "For what?"

"To evaluate his cognition."

"What do you mean?"

"To see whether it might be prudent to consider another living arrangement."

"Like a nursing home? He definitely doesn't need that. He'd never—"

"Your father is functioning independently now. But there are options, if after the assessment you feel different. Assisted living facilities with a range of dependency levels."

"I don't…no, he doesn't want something like that."

Dr. Michaelson's expression was hard to read, but Will had the feeling he should remain on guard.

"Have you noticed any confusion?" the doctor asked.

Will thought of his father in the diner, but he'd always been half-present, half-listening. He shook his head. "No."

"Forgetfulness with basic tasks?" the doctor prodded.

Will crossed his arms. "He seems just fine. Same as ever."

The doctor nodded, jotted down another note.

"He cuts hair at the salon in the mall," Will said, unsure why he was defending his father. "He's actually going into work today," he said, though he knew this wasn't true.

"You live out of town?"

"Chicago."

"Any other relatives in this area?"

Will shook his head.

"Since I'm not your father's primary care physician, I don't have his records, but from our short visit today, I think an assessment would be an appropriate recommendation. We can help set up an appointment here, or if you'd rather talk to his primary care doctor, you can do that, too."

"I'll call his primary."

Dr. Michaelson shut the chart, satisfied. "Very good."

Will stood up. "Thanks for fixing his thumb."

"I can have Marsha up front give you some information. There are some very good facilities around here."

Will returned to the waiting room. He walked right past Marsha at reception readying her materials to give him. His father was sleeping in the waiting room's chair.

"Come on, Dad," he said, and his father pushed quickly to his feet. "Let's get out of here."

His father was struggling with the seatbelt. Will leaned over to help. Up close, he could hear the rattle of his breath. His father smelled like coffee. He had always smelled like coffee.

Will pulled forward, driving below the limit, both hands on the wheel.

They were quiet in the car. The news radio filled the space. His father was falling asleep. A prescription container stuck halfway from his pant pocket. As soon as Will got back to Chicago, he would call his father. With the ease of long distance, he would ask for the name and number of his father's doctor. He could arrange an appointment from afar. Everything would be fine. He could always fly back. No reason to bother his father now. Will lowered the radio.

Outside the apartment complex, Will parked in the spot marked for visitors. He opened the passenger side door, but his father scolded him. "Go on, get back in the car, you've got to get to the airport now."

"Come on." Will stayed there until his father got out of the car.

"Well," he said once his father regained himself. He had an urge to apologize. "Take care of your thumb. What'd they tell you? Keep it dry?"

"Agh, what do they know?" He gave a two-fingered salute, then held his good hand out for a shake.

"I'll call when I get home," Will said. When he shook his father's hand, he felt something folded against his palm. He pulled his hand away. A fifty-dollar bill was pressed into Will's palm, crisply folded in thirds.

"No, Dad, please. I don't need your money," Will said, but his father was already walking away.

Will held open his hand like it hurt, the folded bill stuck to it like an injury. He watched his father, elbows crooked out like they did, walking away in his familiar, uneven strides.

Halfway across the lot, his father held up a hand, and without turning back, called, "Say hello."

Will knew he was referring to that young woman his son married whose name he could not remember right now.

To who? Will wanted to call back, challenge him.

But instead, he shouted, "I will." A promise, like he meant it.

"I will," he said again, this time after his father had already gone.

II.

Airways

Will couldn't sleep. Rain blew heavy against the bedroom window. The clanking was worsening with the storm, the gutter beating madly against the side of the house. Every damn clank reminding him of the mid-years of his life—his second wife sleeping soundly beside him, their first baby slowly growing inside her pregnant belly—and of the man he was supposed to be.

A crash of thunder, then another angry whack from the broken gutter. He'd have to do something. Bethany slept soundly beside him. Six-and-a-half months pregnant and the half moon of her belly matched her swollen breasts. Her legs and arms were slender with her tennis muscles. Will sucked in his gut which had begun to sag over the band of his underwear.

The storm picked up. A roar of thunder and a high moan pressed against the pane. Between each clunk came intermittent pings. *Clink, clank, ping.* Like coins tossed into an empty well, slipping from his hold, mocking him for what he and the rain, but not yet Bethany, knew the outcome would be—Will would call for an estimate, which would be too much, and after a short argument when Bethany would tell him how little time they'd have once the baby came, he would end up calling his ex-brother-in-law Fred to see if he had a friend.

Bethany began to snore. It was another development with the pregnancy that had started a few weeks ago whenever she slept on her back. Something to do with airways, she had explained. The pressure from her uterus on her stomach on her lungs, or maybe her throat, he couldn't remember. It was common and would go away, she reassured him. But he was honest when he told her it didn't bother him. Another one of the buoyant things that rose after the divorce to reveal a small fact about himself; he was a man who wasn't bothered when his pregnant wife snored. It was something he took note of, as if studying the ways and habits of the man he was now.

He was supposed to nudge her if she rolled onto her back, but he let her sleep. One arm draped across her forehead, her natural blonde hair cascading off the pillow, one hand on her stomach, protecting.

Will searched for his slippers. The monstrous gutter blew away from the house then back at it, slamming into the siding. It hung suspended by a twist of metal, dangling a couple of feet over the small section of slanted roof outside their bedroom window. It was as if the gutter were calling out his failures to have done anything to fix it yet. Another thunderous roar, this time followed by a shock of lightening, and the arm swung dangerously towards the glass. "Crap," he whispered, finding his slippers in the dark. He hurried downstairs to look for some twine.

The gutters, the suburban house, the pregnancy: all this was new. It was hard to remember how he and his first wife, Linda, had spent five years of marriage. They had rented a high-rise condo in the Loop overlooking Lake Michigan. They entertained—cocktail parties, mostly charming Linda's clients. After they were finally divorced, Will met Bethany online—*thirty-four-year-old woman enjoys helping others, cooking, traveling, watching foreign films, and working as a receptionist in a doctor's office.* She contacted him first. *Forty-year-old male seeks companionship, tennis (tennis player not required), the movies, etc…I am kind and successful.* Fred was the one who wrote the profile for Will, and Will assumed it was his way of apologizing for his sister's behavior, though Will never blamed him for Linda. Linda was just Linda. It was Will who'd been the fool to think otherwise.

The first thing Bethany asked about when they talked on the phone was movies—*which was his favorite? Did he like foreign films, too? Funny, not too many people mentioned the movies anymore*…And when she pressed him for his all-time favorite, she sounded so sincere about the whole thing that Will didn't have the heart to tell her that he couldn't remember the last time he'd gone to the movies. He glanced out his apartment window and saw a city bus wrapped with an advertisement for an animated movie. He read her the title.

She asked if it was a re-make of a 1960's film starring Paul Newman. He told her it was just a silly kids' movie. The bus disappeared, and Will asked to take Bethany to dinner.

She told Will she liked the way he sounded on the phone. He sounded available, in the real sense of the word. Six months later, when she showed him the blue plus sign on the plastic stick, Bethany found the name of a realtor. The rest happened quickly. Moving to the western suburbs of Chicago, into a modest two-story house with wall-to-wall carpeting, a baby room already painted yellow, and a two-car attached garage.

Will stood in the garage now and looked around for twine. He checked the pantry closet. No luck. He picked up a pile of mail from the kitchen table. A brochure from a local senior living facility was addressed to Bethany, despite Will's father's refusal to leave Florida. Just the gesture—getting the brochure—made Bethany something Will wasn't. "I'm gathering information," she had explained, "maybe down the road."

He had bills to pay. Nothing "down the road" about that. Here was cable (for Bethany's movies), here was electric, and water. He'd never paid for water in the city. Water. Gutters. Work. Will told himself not to think about Gabe—the young manager informing him there'd be cut-backs in winter, but not to worry, he was pretty sure Will's job was safe. Seniority and all. But you know, the economy, Gabe had said.

The Economy. Everyone said this the same way. Like cancer or some new disease people were afraid to talk about for fear of being afflicted. The Economy: a deliberate nod, knowing what this meant, for everybody else. Gabe knew nothing about the baby coming in less than three months, or the broken gutter, or his second wife and the metamorphosis inside her. Metamorphosis, hypothesis, apocalypse: it all sounded the same.

In the garage, on a shelf lined with gallons of old paint, he found a roll of duct tape and some wire hangers. He looked out at the storm. It was past midnight. The gutter swung, twisting like it was trying to break free. He'd secure it until morning. He could hear Linda criticizing him for his ineptitude. Her truths about him resounded as he stood in the open garage wearing his thin pajama pants and matching buttoned top, waiting for the storm to pass. The roll of duct tape and two wire hangers in hand, his only defense.

The idea of children and a house in the suburbs had sounded like a *real* marriage. It was part of the untangling—facts of himself revealed. Like the fact that he hated Maraschino cherries: the medicinal smell; the stickiness on the jar and its permanent red ring in the fridge; the way it'd float in his martini glass like an obstruction, knocking into his lips whenever he took a drink; the irresistible way Linda would twist the tail of its stem between her fingers, rolling the cherry inside her mouth, pressing her perfect teeth lightly into the red skins without breaking through; the way she did this while various clients milled about their condo, enjoying the view. After the divorce, Will vowed never to buy another jar. That was one thing. The other was children. Sure, he wouldn't mind a kid or two.

Bethany was like moving to another country. He could become anyone.

After one grand finale, the thunder stopped, and the rain slowed. Will propped the ladder against the side of the house. "Don't fall," he pleaded with the gutter. His voice fell flat in the night. He slid his wrist through the roll of duct tape, tucked the hangers into the back of his pajama pants, and started to climb.

"If you could see me now," he said, concentrating on the wobbling ladder as he inched to the second rung. "Dear Linda, is this *man* enough for you? Did Jones, or whatever his name was…what kind of name is that anyway?...did your *fellow* ever climb an actual ladder?" Will wiped his hands on his pajama top and re-gripped. He stepped carefully to the next rung. "In the *rain*, for God's sake?" he shook his head. "No, I'm sure he never did." He stopped to catch his breath and rearranged the hangers, squeezing the hooks over his waistband. The drizzle fell gently over his face as he turned his eyes to the sky.

The gutter was daring to tear off and bounce over the roof's edge, knocking Will and his ladder down with him. "Your man ever fix with his own goddamn hands, a *gutter*? You probably don't even know what that means, do you? You probably think it sounds quaint and old-fashioned like everything else that is normally expected out of general members of society…like making a family. Whoever gave *you* a free pass out of decent human behavior?"

Will's heart was pounding so fast, he thought it might trip into some kind of arrhythmia. He inhaled deeply and blew out slowly through his pursed lips like Bethany had taught him to do. Something she learned in a child-birthing class on how to breathe during labor. She wanted to go natural. Give it a try at least. She was going to hire a woman to be with them in the hospital room during the whole thing, which Will thought sounded a little strange, but who was he to say? He'd do whatever she wanted—breathe in, blow out, press the spot between her thumb and forefinger which she said was supposed to relieve pain.

He pulled himself gingerly to the top rung and threw his weight over the slanted roof. His cotton pajamas stuck to his skin. His slippers were soaked. He lay on his stomach, resting his face against the shingles, then scooted himself forward, inching on his elbows so he wouldn't slip.

But just then, his foot knocked against the ladder. "No," he cried, but it already was swaying away from the house. Before Will could sit up, the ladder clattered with a loud crash onto the driveway.

"Oh, shut up," Will cursed Linda's voice. He dropped his face back onto the shingles and swore. The hangers poked his skin. He pulled them from his pants and scooted himself upright. The gutter hung in front of him, eye to eye. With a gust of wind, it took a sharp swing at Will's head. He ducked just in time, and it smacked into the siding. Will exhaled, sitting back against the house.

A light turned on at the Murphy's house across the street. The front door cracked open, and Lois Murphy peered into the night, clutching her silk bathrobe at her chest. She'd heard the ruckus, no doubt.

"Sorry, just dropped my ladder," Will called.

But she didn't hear him. She opened her door wider, and another figure slipped out. Was that Garrison from down the block? Jack Murphy's car wasn't in the driveway. Jack traveled often. They embraced and then Lois and Garrison were kissing.

"Oh, for fuck's sake," Will said, with sickening regret.

They waved silently goodbye. Garrison started down the Murphy's front walkway, toward his own house, five doors down the street, where his wife slept along with his two teenaged daughters who had recently offered to be babysitters when the baby came.

Will wished he hadn't seen that. Garrison crossed the empty street. A panic came over Will; he needed his ladder. He couldn't break the window, and it was too high to jump.

"Hey," Will called.

But Garrison kept walking, hunched in the drizzle.

"Gary," Will called. "Garrison Wallingford."

Garrison froze in his tracks and jerked around. For a moment, Will realized the power in his position, he could scare the hell out of him, make him think some invisible ghost was shouting his name from the sky, ready to strike him down. But really, Will needed his ladder.

"I'm up here. On my roof," Will called through cupped hands.

Garrison walked back towards Will's driveway. The automatic light came on, illuminating Garrison's bewildered face.

"That you, Will?"

"I've got a bit of a problem here." He saw Garrison calculate the situation and realize what Will must have witnessed. "I need my ladder."

"I was....taking a walk...couldn't sleep, you know," he stuttered as he hoisted the ladder against the house. "That the gutter?"

"Yup."

Garrison was crawling up. He was faster than Will, his athletic body taking each rung, effortlessly. He propped his elbows on the rooftop. "Oh, that's bad," he said. "I'll help you, man."

"No need. I got it."

Garrison stayed leaning over the edge of the roof as Will began to work off a long strand of duct tape.

"Bethany coming along?"

"Six months," Will said, tearing the tape with his teeth.

"That's great." Garrison feigned enthusiasm.

"Go home," Will said.

Garrison looked back at the Murphy's house. It was in plain sight. "Marissa and I..."

Will held up his hand. "Not my business."

Garrison let out a long exhale. "We're going through some things."

Will tore off another strand of tape. It felt good to be doing something.

"Shit." Garrison wiped his face.

"Go home," Will said. He picked up a hanger and began untwisting the wire neck. "Thanks for grabbing my ladder."

Garrison nodded. He watched Will untwist the second hanger.

"You gonna rig it up?"

"Something like that."

Garrison thumped a fist against the shingles. Will pulled off another longer piece of duct tape, tearing it between his teeth. He and Garrison never had much interaction more than the neighborly hellos. He didn't want to start now.

"Go home," he said again this time with more force.

"Yeah." Garrison retreated quietly down the ladder and disappeared into the dark.

Will tore one last piece of tape biting down harder than necessary. Through the rain covered window, Bethany slept. He wanted to be back inside beside her while it was still just the two of them. Who would this child be? In a few short months, they would have a baby. Will would be a father. Who was to say what anybody's best consisted of? He practiced Bethany's breathing again.

He found his balance and hoisted the gutter up to its natural position. The collected rain spilled, dripping into Will's sleeves. He wrapped the wire hangers around the gutter like a sling and fastened it to the top. He took each piece of duct tape and pressed firmly until the gutter held intact. It would stay, at least until morning.

Bethany was still on her back, snoring. With the swell of each progressing month, a force-field grew around her, drew her inside its echoing chambers, so that whenever Will felt the urge to reach for her, it was the baby again between them.

Her nightstand held a rising stack of baby name books, pages marked with her favorites—Ruby or Riley for a girl, Hunter or Jason for a boy—beside various tubs of lotion and creams, lip balm, and her oversized water bottle covered with pink flowers. His nightstand held a digital clock. It was 2:17 a.m.

He stood in a dark corner of the bedroom, removed his drenched pajamas, and dropped them in a pile by his feet. He wiped himself off with a towel. The rain was starting up again, hitting the rigged gutter just enough to make it rattle. In the morning, he would call Fred. He would call Fred before Bethany asked anything about it. He wondered if everyone kept secrets from their loved ones. The thought of Garrison and Lois made him queasy. He wished he hadn't seen that. He didn't want to know their secret. Who was he to know what went on behind someone else's closed door? Wasn't that where life was at its messiest?

Bethany was awake. She sat up, moving her long hair away from her sleepy face. Her breasts hung down resting on the ball of her stomach. Her nipples had darkened along with a mysterious line running down the middle of her belly. A thick blue vein bulged across her chest. Everything in her seemed to pulse. She pulled the sheet up to the base of her pubic bone, right beneath the moon.

"You ok, Babe?"

He liked that she called him this. It was never Honey. Honey was what Linda used. Everybody to Linda was Honey—the girl who came to wash the carpets, the doorman, her clients, Will. Babe was part of the new country. The man he was in Bethany's world.

"You were on your back."

"Oh god, snoring?"

Will shook his head. This was another thing: it wasn't hard to lie. Maraschino cherries, children, lying. They floated to the surface. Existed, for better or worse.

She yawned a big slow yawn without covering her mouth.

The gutter sounded outside the window.

"Is that rain?"

He put his arm out as though he could cover the noise, keep her from knowing who he was, who she'd married, that he hadn't yet gotten to the quote or the argument or the phone call. It was like the ghost of himself with Linda followed him here into this new country with Bethany.

"You should sleep," he said.

"Why are you up?"

"I'm not."

"Are you naked?" she said, squinting into the darkness.

"I was hot." He kicked the wet pile of pajamas to the side.

"Come to bed." She patted the mattress and lay back down.

He crossed the room and touched the sheet with her foot veiled beneath it. She stretched out her legs, curling onto her left side.

Her voice was quiet, facing the curtains. "Come here," she said, and rolled slightly to look at him over her shoulder. From behind, it was hard to see the pregnancy. He crawled onto the bed, the mattress sinking under his weight. She made a soft sound as Will curled close behind. She reached back for his arm, brought it to rest on her hip. He brought his face to the crevice of her neck, and her own hands settled back onto the moon. He kissed her shoulder, tasting the salt on her skin. It reminded him of nothing, and something about this comforted him.

The rain grew stronger, steadier. The clinking resumed, but it was contained. Will felt a small rise of satisfaction at having rigged it up. This was his job, and he'd do it right. In the morning, he'd finally take care of the damn thing for real, first thing.

"I hope the rain stops," Bethany murmured. After a moment, a hint of her snore returned. Will tapped her gently, her snoring paused.

"Gutter guy's supposed to come in the morning," she muttered softly into her pillow.

He pulled back. "What?" he whispered.

Maybe he'd misunderstood. It was late. It was dark. He'd barely heard her. Maybe she said *the sun's supposed to be out in the morning,* or something else completely.

But she had already started to breathe the heavy breath of sleep.

It was too early to determine, the obstetrician had said at one of their first visits when Will, sitting in the small metal chair pressed against the wall behind the paper-covered examining table, asked *boy or girl?* Not that he had a preference. A baby was a baby. But he had wanted to ask the doctor a question, show her he was involved, that he was the kind of man who asked his pregnant wife's obstetrician a question. He noticed a brief exchange between Bethany and the doctor, something that made Will feel acutely aware of himself in the way one does when watching another man watch the cherry roll between your wife's perfect teeth or lying beside your second wife's naked body while another heart beats and grows inside of her.

So a gutter guy would come. Did it matter? Maybe everyone should just open their doors and release the pressure. Maybe once you saw whatever it was you saw, then there was nothing really left to complain about.

Either way, whether she knew it yet or not, he'd prove to her he was worth holding onto.

It didn't take long before her snoring grew louder, this time while on her side, and something about it relaxed him. He stayed close and kept his face in her hair. He lay awake listening to the sound of her pregnant snore as though it were a lifeline, joining him to her, the narrowing airways caused by the expanding uterus pressing onto the stomach or the lungs or the bronchial tubes or something, and this was all right. This was a place he could stay, on this stream of breath sliding through the constriction, while the world simultaneously swelled and contracted around him.

III.

Arboretum

Three months had passed since Will last visited his father in the Arboretum. This time, he flew down without his wife and son on a last-minute ticket after the call from the director informing him that his father had punched a ninety-one-year-old resident in the face. She needed to discuss the possibility of relocating him to the B-wing. Will didn't want his father moved to the B-wing. He was dreading the trip, unsure how to help, but here he was now, the smell of antiseptic striking him as soon as he stepped into Riverview Assisted Living. He passed down the long corridor to the memory care wing.

He knew that as soon as he entered the room, his father would be sitting in the recliner chair, watching the TV that would be on too loud; he knew his legs would be splayed apart on the footrest raised to its maximum height, and that his slippers would be propped around his swollen feet. The curtain would be drawn, the blinds closed, and he was ready for the stench made worse by the turned-up heat. But what Will didn't expect was how different his father would look.

He sat in his chair like something overgrown. His fine silver hair nearly brushed the tops of his shoulders, and his face was covered in ashy stubble. He looked like he had become part of the room, like something rising from the carpet or the cushions of the chair.

Will froze in the threshold.

"Dad?"

Nothing.

The TV played a barrage of images from an entertainment news station, overlapping with the announcer's frenetic voice.

"What's going on here?" Will found the remote hanging from the recliner's armrest and lowered the volume.

"Shut the door. You're letting in a draft," his father muttered. A familiar voice now coming from a stranger.

"Hey, it's me, Dad." Will leaned down to kiss him on the cheek. It was something he'd never felt before—the stubble on his father's face.

A flicker of recognition, Will saw it, yes, of course, he still knew his son.

Will sat on the bed covered with the same red plaid blanket his father had always used. He unbuttoned his shirt's collar, then rolled up his sleeves. "You have breakfast?"

Breakfast, it was always breakfast with them. But by 8 a.m., the dining room was already being cleared. He had noticed a woman wearing a thin robe, head hung over a sippy cup—the kind Max used to drink from—and he wondered if she might be the ninety-one-year-old resident, Brenda Thatcher, who his father had hit when she wandered into the wrong room.

At the mention of breakfast, his father looked up at Will with surprise.

"Where you at now?" The same question he always asked.

"Chicago, Dad. I'm still in Chicago."

"Oh, yeah?"

Will wanted to ask his father why the hell he looked like a gray wolf, why they'd stopped grooming him, why they'd apparently left him here to rot.

Just then the door opened and a heavy-set nurse with tightly pulled back hair entered the room. "Hello, there," she said too loudly.

His father was visibly startled. "Get the hell outta here."

Will stood and reached for his father's shoulder.

"You've got to take these here," the nurse said in a lilting accent, ignoring the outburst. She held out a small paper cup of pills. His father swatted the air, hitting the cup out of her hand, causing the pills to go flying across the rug.

"Dad!" Will scolded. "Sorry," he said and bent down to collect the pills.

The aide held up both hands in surrender. "Mr. Leonard, nobody's going to hurt you." She made a tsk'ing sound and left the room.

His father turned stone-faced; the sagging skin quivered slightly beneath his chin.

Will set the cup of pills on the desk and exhaled deeply. "It's OK," he said. "It's fine." Though he wasn't sure if he was comforting his father or himself.

He imagined Brenda Thatcher wandering into the room like an intruder, opening the wardrobe. He wasn't sure how much his father remembered of the incident. He wanted to tell his father that he'd make it right. He'd come here to help, after all. Nobody wanted to get moved to the B-wing. So why couldn't everyone just stay out of each other's rooms?

The handwritten list Bethany had made a few months ago still hung on the wall. It read: Will=your son; Bethany=Will's wife (your daughter-in-law); Max=your grandson (3 yrs. old). It was an idea she had read about. Both her parents were alive and well on the west coast.

Will removed a photograph of his son from his wallet and held it out to his father. The last time they came to visit, Max played with a Hot Wheels car, pulling apart blinds behind the bed and making the car nosedive along the panels, and his father had found it amusing.

"Look at your grandson. Max." It was from his birthday party last week, eating cake, looking adorable in his paper hat. "He just turned four."

His father looked at the picture and it seemed to clear some fog and calm him down.

"Put it with the others." He pointed at the lampshade covered with photographs taped to it from when he'd still lived in his apartment. Will turned the shade around the lamp and found a space beside a picture of his mother and father posing with Goofy.

When his parents had moved to Orlando after his mother became ill, their new condo quickly filled with everything Disney. Miniature glass figurines lined the living room mantel beneath a sign that read *Never Stop Dreaming.* In the kitchen, another sign read *Smiles are as Good as Bacon!* Everything demanded happiness, and it had made Will uncomfortable when he visited. In the photograph, Goofy's oversized white gloves were wrapped around their shoulders like a proud cartoon dad. His parents were smiling like they'd won a prize, like the enormous dog in his tall, rumpled hat was real. Will fastened the picture of Max beside it on the lampshade.

"Mr. Leonard?" A sing-song voice came from the doorway. A smaller woman wearing a brightly patterned nursing shirt stepped into the warm room. "You giving Ruby a hard time I hear?" Her nametag read *Serena.*

"He got upset—I don't know why," Will said.

"We're all together, Mr. Leonard. Nobody wants to hurt you," she said.

Will wanted to tell her there was nothing wrong with his father's hearing.

"You've got to take these now." She held out the palmful of pills with a cup of water. The smell and heat in the room made Will nauseous. His father obeyed and swallowed.

He was barely recognizable. His father, who used to tuck his bedsheets without a crease, who had managed the hair salon in the mall and taught Will about geometrical precision, the importance of a clean bathroom and clipped nose hairs, now looked like an overgrown weed.

"Why's his hair so long?" Will asked the nurse.

"He won't let us touch him. It happens." Then more loudly to his father, "It's OK, Mr. Leonard."

But it was not OK. Will had never seen his father unkempt. He could remember being a young boy trying to lay out his clothes the same way his father did each morning with trained precision. Once he saw his father ironing, releasing steam onto the shirt pinned beneath, and even in his undershirt, his father had total command, each hair neatly combed in place, each wrinkle quietly extinguished before it even had a chance.

He had to do something. He'd talk with the director.

"I need my log book," his father said.

"You want a book?" Serena said.

"It's a notebook—something he used to track finances in," Will explained.

"You don't need money here. Everything's free here, Mr. Leonard. It all free free free." She waved her open palms.

Will cringed at the lie. If his father knew that Will had taken a home equity loan to help cover the costs, he would not have approved. Riverview was known for its memory care, but given his father's state now, Will was concerned.

When the nurse left the room, Will yanked the mini-fridge's plug to stop the annoying buzzing it was making. The same unopened carton of milk from three months ago sat inside. Last visit, his father had been puzzling over the lack of a refrigerator. "What if the boy wants a glass of milk?" He was talking about Max. "You want some milk?" Max shook his head, driving his Hot Wheels through the blinds.

"They have whatever you want here," Will had told his father. "Right outside your door."

"Sometimes one wants a glass of milk," his father had said.

That was all it took for Bethany to drive to Walmart, despite there being no need for a refrigerator in his room.

He would remove it today.

His father pointed to the large plastic wall clock. "You know they've got two of them on there?"

It was the same clock that used to hang in his parents' kitchen. The one Will had taken the batteries out of after his mother's funeral. He and his father were sitting at the kitchen table, waiting for water to boil on the stove, when his father said with a pained look, "has that thing always ticked so loud?" as though it offended him. Will had dragged a chair over to stand on it and then he removed the batteries, and when he turned back around, he thought he saw his father wipe a tear before he pushed away from the table.

"I don't know what you mean," Will said now.

"They've got three in the day and again three in the night."

It was hard to see his father like this. He wanted to apologize. He wanted to dust off the webs from his father's mind, give him back the sharp edges of his memories. It was like Max and his inability to grasp time—*how many minutes is five? How much time is that? When is nine o'clock?*

Will reached for the remote. "It's just the time, Dad."

He pulled open the heavy curtain. The stark sun pierced through the glass. "Maybe if you got some air in here."

"They got that over by you, too?"

"Huh?" He tried to open the window, but it was sealed. "Yeah, we've got it," Will said. "They have it everywhere. It's just how it is."

"Where you at now?"

He raised the volume slightly to distract his father back into the comfortable distance from the things he once knew. "Still in Chicago, Dad."

His father shut his eyes. The flashing lights from the TV fell over him, soothing him back into the place he went, washed over by sounds and colors and absence.

At the nurses' station, Will waited for an aide to come by. He noticed an old woman sitting alone in the corner of the common room on a blue couch beside a dollhouse. She was wrapping and unwrapping a shawl around her narrow shoulders. He wondered if it was Brenda Thatcher.

She looked just fine. All the trouble his father was in, warnings of the B-wing, new medication, and there she sat, perfectly intact like an old dandelion. Maybe someone should remind her not to enter someone else's room, tell *her* about the B-wing.

A hissing startled him. It was a resident he remembered from his last visit. He was walking frenzied laps around the floor, hissing between his teeth as though he were trying to expel something. He had scared Max when he came toward him, reaching for his youth like he wanted to swoop him up. Will had brought Max back to his father's room and shut the door with its numeric pad programmed with the same 1-2-3 codes that did not actually lock the doors, but was an illusion of comfort, the supervisor had explained, which Will thought should do more to keep the residents out of each other's rooms.

Light as a ghost, a hand was on his back. He jumped and turned. The old woman stood close behind Will now, the top of her head rising to the center of his chest.

"Arthur?" she said, looking up at him with hopeful anticipation. Her glassy eyes were dark holes beneath folds of wrinkles as she searched his face for recognition. "Is that you?" Her dry lips were covered with a white film. She rested her skeletal hand on Will's arm.

"I'm sorry," Will said, shaking his head.

"Arthur," she breathed, her voice barely audible, as though there was not enough force to carry it across the short distance between them. Then she rested her head against Will's chest. He could see the top of her pink skull. She smelled like vinegar. They could have been poised for a slow dance. Will froze, scanning the room for an aide.

She peered up at him again, and he looked for any sign of bruising on her face, but there was none. His father could not have hit her hard. He had never hit anyone before.

His arms hung heavy by his sides. He tried to step with her back toward the couch but was afraid she might fall. The common room was empty aside from the hisser rounding his laps.

"You've come," she said with such relief, and he felt her surrender, resting her fragile head against him.

He patted her lightly. "It's OK. It's fine," he said. He knew it was her. He knew it was Brenda Thatcher. Finally, a nurse approached and extracted her by the elbow, gently returning her to the blue couch without a word.

A male aide pushed his cart carrying little paper cups along the corridor, and Will asked him for a pair of grooming scissors. He said he'd be right back.

"Hello, Mr. Leonard." The director found him in the hall. She held out her hand to shake. She wore a royal blue suit and a yellow blouse, and her expression was pinched as though trying to smile through something sour. "I'm glad to have the chance to talk with you. How is your father doing today?"

It dawned on him that his father's outburst, knocking the pills from the nurse's hand, hadn't reached the director yet.

"He seems alright," Will said. Then before she could talk about the offense, he added, "he hasn't had a haircut or a shave for some time."

She nodded, the sour rising to the surface. "It's the increased agitation. He won't allow anyone close enough to shave or trim his hair. It happens." She explained a new medication meant to curtail aggressive or unpredictable behavior. It bothered Will how she talked. His father was not some kind of wild animal.

His father had always been in charge. Growing up, each day of the week had its own assignment according to his father. Saturdays were lawn day. Wednesdays were TV dinners. Fridays meant haircuts. Every Friday, Will's father would wash and trim the family's hair in the washer basin his father had installed in their basement. Will hated that sink—it hurt his neck, and the menthol bite of shampoo from the oversized jugs, and the icy water, and his father's rough hands on his skull. Will told his classmates he went to the regular barber in town like everyone else, but they recognized a "Mr. Leonard cut," which was too short, too exact.

When Will went to college, he grew his hair just over his ears, and though he came home every weekend, Fridays were no longer family haircutting day, and his father declared college a scam if they let kids go scruffy like that.

"The new medication will help sedate his nerves," the director told Will. "But we have recorded it as Level One Watch."

He didn't know Level One Watch, but he did know the B-wing. Riverview was shaped like an octopus, a central rotunda which branched into multiple corridors leading to different wings. The Arboretum, where his father stayed, was the A-wing, for memory care. The B-wing was closed off with a security door. When they first toured Riverview, the supervisor didn't take them to that wing, but Will remembered him using words like "progressive deterioration" and "tranquilize," which made Bethany squeeze Will's hand.

"I don't want my father moved to the B-wing. Please give him another chance."

The director nodded. "Given it's your father's first offence. We can keep him on Level One Watch. But if another incident occurs, we will have to reconsider. We must keep everyone safe, and of course we think about the good for all our residents."

Will swallowed a bitter taste in his throat. "Right."

The director left him in the hall. The aide finally returned and handed him a small pair of scissors.

"Patients can't have these, so be sure to return them to me," he said, pushing his cart down the carpeted hall.

"Will do, thank you," Will said to no one.

When he returned to the room, his father was asleep in the chair, hands folded gently in his lap, the TV flashing disco over his ashen face. The sun seemed offensive now. He pulled shut the heavy curtain.

From the adjoining bathroom, Will took two rough hand towels and a plastic comb and brought them to his father's recliner. He laid one of the towels on the carpet. He draped the other towel over his father's shoulders. His bones jutted out beneath the brown sweater.

"You know what I don't like?" his father said suddenly.

It startled Will. His father slid between sleep and wake so seamlessly.

"What's that, Dad?" He stood behind the chair. He was glad his father knew it was still him, some memory intact, a root that was thicker than others, that connected him to his only son. His father wouldn't think him an intruder, even if he entered the room in the middle of a deep sleep, and this felt like some kind of victory.

"Here, sit forward a minute, will you, Dad?" He straightened the towel across his father's shoulders.

"You notice they don't have any doors on that thing? Shouldn't they have doors?"

He was talking about the bathroom. Will had heard the complaint before.

"I'm going to sit you upright." Will pressed the recliner's remote.

"I like to lean."

"I'll put you back when I'm done."

His father didn't respond. Used to succumbing now. Take this pill, drink this water.

"I'm going to cut your hair, Dad. Just sit still. You can relax."

His father kept his head down, chin resting on chest like he knew what to do. This, after all, was his father's world. Thirty years in a salon.

Will took a deep breath. He'd never done anything like this before. He combed the thin gray strands at the base of his father's skull, down over his neck. He took the scissors and made the first snip carefully across the bottom. The hair fell silently onto the towel. He waited to see if his father would move or say something. But he was quiet. Holding perfectly still, hands folded.

Will could remember being a boy, sitting in the oversized swirly chair while his father told him to quit his squirming. He snipped the scissors again across the bottom, bending down to see if he was cutting it evenly. Tried to remember anything his father might've taught him about cutting hair, but all he could remember was his father saying you've got to sit still.

Will drew the comb gently along the side of his father's head above his ear and snipped. Wisps of hair dropped onto the towel. A light snore sounded from his father's back.

He continued around the other side, behind that ear. His father sat motionless, expertly. Even in his sleep, he knew what to do.

This was the most he had ever touched his father's hair, his head, his neck and shoulders. Never before did Will understand the intimacy in putting your hands in someone else's hair. The fact that his father spent his life doing this was a mystery to him now.

He dusted some loose hairs off the sleeve of his father's sweater.

It wasn't perfect. But at least it was cleaned up. He gathered the edges of the towel from his father's shoulders, careful to cradle the loose hairs, careful not to jar him awake.

"Now take the top," his father instructed.

It startled Will again. "Jesus, I thought you were sleeping."

He stood holding the balled-up towel like he'd been caught. "I'm done," he said.

His kept his position perfectly still, waiting.

"Take the top," his father repeated. "Comb it forward, then lift straight up with your fingers," he said into his chest. There was command in his father's voice, a sudden clarity. "Lift up and cut like that. Real close. Use two fingers."

His father sat stone steady. Back in the salon. Training his employees to cut hair.

The old version of his father was still in there, and moments like this when it rose through the murk, Will wanted to grab hold of who he was before he slipped away again.

Will set the towel back on the floor. He took the comb and did as his father said. He drew it forward over the top of his head, lifting the hair between his two fingers and snipped across, real close.

"That's right," his father murmured.

Will's face warmed. He dropped the hairs from the back of his hand onto the floor. A few pieces landed on his shoe. Again, he brought the comb to the crown of his father's head, drew it forward, lifted, snipped. The silver strands falling.

"That's right," his father murmured again as Will continued slow and steady, "that's right, just like that…that's right…" his father's voice low and calm as though soothing a baby.

The Children Will Perform at the Gala

They want us to perform for the rich people, play our violins, read our poems, stepdance. We are kept in a holding room lined with uncomfortable chairs, a pitcher of water and a plate of cookies on a table against the wall. We are told to wait. There is nothing to do. We push each other around but get bored. We slump against the wall in the fancy clothes they told us to wear. Hours later, they come for us.

We are led past the ballroom, where tables are covered with white tablecloths. The room is full of voices, laughter, dresses that glitter.

They move us into the kitchen area, where workers are hurried and serious and worried when they see us young people lined up in their space, sure we will destroy something important. They tell us to be careful of sharp corners, delicate objects, not to touch a thing. Their eyes are telling us *go away*. We pass trays lined with chocolate cakes. Half domes drizzled with shiny white glaze. Each cake sits upon a paper doily. It looks like a village of miniature igloos. Behind our paper masks, our mouths fall open. Our breathing slows. They respond firmly, confirming none are for us. They take us out the back door and into another small waiting area by a side entrance to the ballroom. We feel like thieves, hiding out, but maybe, we think, this is what it feels like to be important. We are hushed even though we are not speaking. We stay hidden, waiting our turn to entertain.

We peek through the crack. The rich people are eating their dinners, drinking glassfuls of sparkly champagne. They are clapping for the young people playing their brass instruments on the stage.

We are so still, we barely breath. They tell us again to hush. They tell us to behave, this is an honor, fix our hair, not everybody gets to perform, they remind us. We nod and look down apologizing, unsure what we are sorry for.

A woman on stage is now talking about how she used to be homeless. She is a large woman wearing a multicolor silky dress wrapped around her thick middle, and she leans onto the podium with both elbows. The rich people are crying. The used-to-be-homeless woman tells them she struggled with anxiety and depression when she lived on the streets, but now she feels much better. The people are nodding. She tells them she wants to be a social worker one day. The person in charge of us checks her piece of paper, taps her watch. When the woman on stage stops talking, the audience stand from their seats and clap and clap and cry.

It is our turn. They tell us to pull down our masks. Someone we have never seen before introduces us and tells the crowd we are important, and that we are the voice of the future. We march into the bright room, squinting into the light. The room is enormous. The ceiling too tall. The people are watching, wanting. We do what we are told. We read slowly and clearly. We read the words we have written that our teacher tells us matter, words that will change the world. For three full minutes, our voices in the microphone fill the large room. And they listen to us.

When we finish, we want to run onto the dance floor, sit at the fancy tables, eat all the food. We want to shine with the dresses, drink champagne, laugh. But we are hurried out the side door, back through the kitchen where the chocolate domes have multiplied. Trays everywhere, all of them covered with those individual cakes. Hundreds of them. We are so hungry.

They return us to the holding room. The chairs are upturned now. The cookies gone, the water pitcher empty. A round woman is sleeping on one of the uncomfortable hotel chairs. Nobody knows who she is. We are told to wait here for our parents to take us home.

Our teacher is told to wait in the holding room, too. She is not allowed in the ballroom. We want those little cakes. She checks the hall before sneaking away. Returning with two plates of chocolate domes, she gives us heavy silver forks, and we crowd the tiny plates. She sneaks out again and returns with more. We flock around her like pigeons.

We hide the chocolate lining our mouths when the person in charge returns and tells us it's time to leave. Our job is done. They lead us down the long hall. Do not enter the ballroom, they remind us, though we have not forgotten. Do not make noise. Do not disrupt. They open the side exit, send us down the stairs, into the darkness of the cool night, where our grown-ups are waiting, where the rich people, pleased with our performance and the way our voices filled the room—our words meant to change the world, our words meant for them—will not see our stolen crumbs or how hungry we still are.

Marionette

Samuel tucked his hands into his armpits and pressed the bruise where Faroozi kicked him yesterday at school. It was still tender. "I told Ms. Keller I'm going to be an astronaut," he said to his mother who was relaxing in her beach chair on the narrow terrace of their sixth-floor apartment. Her eyes were closed. A hardcover book lay on the ground. "But Oscar doesn't care about going to the moon. He said so in P.E," Samuel said, moving his finger from bruised to un-bruised and back again, circling the spot.

"Hand me my sunglasses, will you, baby?" his mother said, opening her book.

"Oscar said he doesn't want to be anything, but Ms. Keller made him go to the blue chair. He always has to go to the blue chair."

"I think an astronaut's a fine thing to be," his mother said.

He pressed the bruise and there was Faroozi again, standing with Goose, the big kid on the playground, the first-grade repeater, two feet planted over Samuel on his back beneath the monkey bars. Faroozi, covered with too much hair, already sweating. Goose and the other boys herded around him like a shadow, Samuel didn't know why. With his snotty nose and crazy way he said things with a voice that was always too loud. Faroozi and his herd of boys hung over Samuel squinting at spots of sun in the sky.

The bruise was the size of a penny or a grape. It didn't hurt. Just spidered when he touched it—a tingly feeling. Bruised. Unbruised. Bruised. And Faroozi's voice was loud and deep. "Girl," he spat and then kicked Samuel hard...right...there.

"Pussy," he yelled. The shadow of boys laughed. Samuel clawed two fistfuls of woodchips with his palms. Another kick. A soft thud. Gym shoe in his armpit. Sunspots in his eyes. Laughter fell in bursts then disappeared when he threw the chips.

It was the first time Samuel had been tagged. Samuel, and usually Jimmy McKinnley because of his red hair and matching splattered birthmark that took over half his face, and Hooper because nobody could tell where he was from or if he knew how to talk because he never did, but mostly because of his name. And of course, Paulie because, well, because he was Paulie.

It didn't matter. One day, Samuel told himself, one day...He looked up and pictured himself there, standing on the moon, looking down at their tiny mean heads.

Samuel hadn't told his mother about being bullied. He thought it would make her do the thing she did before she cried, and he didn't like that—her nose scrunched and her chin all wrinkly; it made her face look strange and nothing good came after that, so he didn't say anything.

Probably because he didn't have a dad. That's what Samuel thought. Why he was tagged. At least he had a mom. Not like Tony Peterson. But Tony would never be tagged, probably because everyone knew Nick and Robbie were his big brothers and nobody wanted those toughies against them. It didn't matter, he kept saying to himself now on the terrace looking through the bars, nothing would matter from that far away. From space he wouldn't even hear them laughing.

Maggie took her sunglasses from Samuel and slid them on. She felt the sun warming her face, her bare arms. It was Sunday. All week she had spent wondering about Marcus. Replayed his words and the way he stood in the long line at the bank on his lunch break waiting for her teller booth to be free so he could give her the book. *It reminded me of you,* he said and handed her the hardcover nicely wrapped in bookstore paper. They'd been dating six weeks. This was his first gift. She was curious, then embarrassed when she noticed the tired, on-looking customers watching them, glimpsing this moment into her private life. She started reading the book that same evening. (Yokiko was a young nurse who had come to the United States after working on a Japanese army base. Her younger brother, Wan, had recently arrived in New York from Japan and was struggling with his new life. Halfway into it now, she still wondered why Marcus had thought of her.) All week she read it slowly, searching for clues, as though it might give her clarity to their relationship and where it was heading.

Inside the book's cover, Marcus had written an inscription: *For my sweet marionette* and in parenthesis her real name *(Maggie)*. He told her once about a traveling puppet show in the small town where he had grown up. That it would appear on a street corner every now and then, cranking out some old accordion music from a box atop a bicycle while marionettes would jump and twirl and collide. He told her how much he loved those puppets, dancing from their invisible strings, so certain they were real, believing if he wished hard enough one might dance right out of the box and march home with him.

Marcus was thirty-eight. He had never been married. Didn't have children. He was a friend of a friend of a friend, and he was the first person she had dated in six years since Samuel's father left. She didn't have any contact with her ex, never knew where he'd disappeared to, and had raised Samuel on her own. She wasn't sure how to date or what the rules were anymore.

Big Shit, Samuel thought and checked to see if his mother had somehow heard. But she picked up her book and was inside it now, and the Asian woman on the back cover stared blankly back at Samuel. *Big Shit*, he thought again and tried it louder in his mind. But still the boys circled. Faroozi drooling like a dog. Woodchips in Samuel's palms. Sun spots. The kick.

"Mom?"

She glanced at Samuel before turning another page (128: Yokiko is in her apartment, and the phone is ringing).

"You've got homework, baby?" she said.

He shook his head. Eleven-year-old Rocco from next door was riding his bike on the sidewalk below. Rocco's little sister was drawing with colored chalk on the front steps.

Maybe he would tell her.

128: Yokiko answers the phone, and it is her brother, Wan on the line. He tells her that their father, who is still in Japan, living as a widower, is sick and needs some money and care. *Kabocha,* Wan begins.

"Do you want some cherries? Are you hungry?" Samuel's mother asked from behind the book, the woman on the back cover watching without moving her lips. "Go ahead," she said, holding her hand out to the space between them.

Or maybe he wouldn't tell.

The herd of boys moved off, business done, circling the grounds to follow girls.

The girls giggled, running away, their voices confetti, colorful bits of sound floating up and down as they scattered across the playground. The boys in all their toughness, hovered, unsure how to enter the sphere that surrounded them. "Go away!" the girls shouted, their cotton dresses fluttering.

Under the high-arched monkey bars, his armpit throbbed. "Samu-la, Samu-la, what a girl!" laughter carrying his name away.

The terrace of their sixth-floor apartment overlooked Maple Street. A tree-lined city street. A mix of new and old constructions on the block. A squirrel skittered on a branch, nervously working a nut with its claws. The sun was bright. The occasional passing of a bus sounded from a block away.

Kabocha, Wan begins, and the author explains this is a Japanese kind of pumpkin—a nickname Wan made up for their father when he was six and his sister nine, and they would hide in the attic room looking through cracks in the wooden floor where they could spy their parents arguing. Wan, always trying to make Yokiko laugh, whispered *see,* laughing as they held her face close to the cracks. Blowing dust, he squeezed shut one eye, straining to see their father's face moving in and out of view. *Kabocha, right? Look, it's true! So green and turning bright orange inside like it's going to explode!* The angry voices boomed beneath them, so he spread his body flat against the floor, palming the wood, trying to see. Their father's face, a fat pumpkin on top of his padded body, wobbling from the weight, the heat, an imaginary flame growing a darker shade of green, and inside a brighter shade of orange every time his voice rose. *Kabocha!* Wan cried, blowing out his checks, shaking his head left to right as though it were too heavy, about to fall off, and they'd cover their mouths to mute their laughter.

Kabocha, Wan, now twenty-five years old, says gently on the phone, and Yokiko knows this is serious. *Father needs our care.*

Maggie turned another page. She took a drink of her water. The glass was warm. A bowl of cherries sat on the ground between them and Samuel took one. She slid her bare feet toward the terrace bars.

Yokiko holds the phone with both hands tightly against her ear. *What's the matter with father?*

Below, on Magnolia, a policeman was writing tickets. Samuel closed one eye and held the cherry by its stem over the spot of the policeman. He moved along the short terrace, trying to keep the cherry on top of his cap. He imagined it falling, dropping on his head and painting his police face red. But the policeman went ahead, and the cherry moved off.

Samuel watched his mother's toes press against the terrace bars. They were painted red, like ten bright apples. One, two, three, four, five. Five red apples. But the last ones were so small and wrinkled, he decided they didn't count. Two rotten apples on the end. Eight shiny red apples. Four for you. And four for you.

The cover of the book blocked his mother's face. Samuel moved closer to her bare feet. He pressed his thumb over her big toe, counting one...

Her foot twitched, and she pulled it back. The book fell into her lap. "Sammy, what are you doing?"

He was glad to see his mother's face. Her sunglasses blocked her eyes, but her mouth was smiling.

"Shannon wants to be a ballerina, and Oscar said there weren't real ones, but she brought her costume to show-and-tell and put it on, and Ms. Keller let her wear it to lunch. She wants to go to the moon, too."

Maggie looked at her six-year-old son, at the light spread of freckles across his nose, the almond shape of his eyes, the innocence she often forgot was still so much part of everything he saw. She filled with a familiar, all-consuming rush to protect him, to keep him safe from the dangers and disappointments in life. It was this instinct to zipper and comb and hold out your hand, this leaning forward, that she didn't think Marcus would understand.

"I gave her my helmet, and she said I could wear her tutu if we were on the moon," he continued. "But Oscar said his dad said we can't."

"Why not? You can be whatever you want," she said.

Not that Marcus seemed uninterested.

"Go on in," she said, "and bring out some paper. You can color a picture. Be your astronaut."

She lifted her book, found her place again.

What's the matter with father?

"Go on. Bring some crayons from the kitchen."

What's the matter...

Samuel looked at the book woman's face again. He noticed his mother's fifth wrinkled toenail, the red paint cracked with tiny lines, and he moved his finger toward it, and with one quick tap, pressed it like a button before jumping up to go inside through the sliding door.

How serious is it? Yokiko wants to ask, but the question doesn't seem necessary. She knows from her brother's voice and the way he calls him *father* that it must be bad. She agrees to put her money together with Wan to send to their father in Japan. They will hire him a nurse. But something about this unsettles Yokiko. Wan is on his way over to her apartment on West 83rd Street. He is traveling up from his studio near Battery Park, so she knows she has some time. She puts on a kettle of water for tea, and even though her apartment is perfectly arranged, she starts to straighten.

Inside their single floor apartment, it was quiet. Samuel went into the bathroom and shut the door, turned the skinny silver lock with both his hands. Then he checked for Rita in the mirror. He knew she didn't come today. Rita came on Tuesdays—this he made himself remember after what happened last time, how she snuck up, how he didn't even hear her coming, how she yelled in her loud Spanish voice, and yanked his hands from his mother's drawer, how the drawer came off its rollers and everything went falling, spilling out onto the bathroom floor—it was her fault, he knew that for sure. A hundred tubes of lipstick rolled around their feet. Rita bent down, hugging her wide arms across the floor, sweeping the lipsticks together. They clicked and clattered, and Samuel stood staring. A pink paisley case slipped behind the toilet. He begged it not to move. Smacking her lips together, she dumped the tubes back into his mother's drawer, then pulled his arms too hard over the edge of the sink, stretching them until they reached the faucet, and pressed his hands between her palms as she scrubbed. *No mas, no mas,* she said as she washed his hands under the warm water, squeezing each finger with soap.

So now, he checked the mirror for Rita, looking in every corner of the reflection, and though he didn't see her he thought that Rita came from nowhere all the time. He checked out the bathroom window overlooking the street for her big black hair, maybe even floating, he thought, like a witch. Big Rita and her smoky spine. But nobody was there, and he double-checked the lock then slowly pulled open his mother's drawer of make-up.

Faroozi and his stupid herd. He would forget about them. Draw them away. Go to the moon. Dance. Whatever. They couldn't get him there. Maybe they would never find him ever again.

Maggie pressed her toes against the terrace bars. She reached back to slide shut the screen door.

Yokiko's kettle of tea is now whistling. Wan will be there soon, and Yokiko who just set out a saucer of biscuits, is looking through her kitchen drawer for the right kind of tea, the Japanese tea that she drinks with her brother, the only kind they ever drink together. But she can only find box after box of American herbal tea. Sure that she must have some left somewhere, she pulls out the entire drawer and sets it on the countertop, starting to feel a sense of dread sink through her.

Samuel took out three tubes of lipstick from his mother's bathroom drawer, uncapped them all, and lined them up next to one another so they stood like red and pink soldiers in shiny gold armor. They faced the mirror, and Samuel leaned in close, choosing the brightest pink first, he started at his eyebrow, then down the inner side of his nose, making a circle around his left eye. He rolled the lipstick higher from its tube, and then filled in the circle making sure none of the skin was left undone. Then he took a red, the color of his mother's toes, and rolled it up, watching the pointed wedge of color rise. He drew a mouth larger than his own around his lips, starting beneath his nose and continuing across the middle of his chin. He remembered the show he saw on the TV, and how their faces looked with all their bright colors, flying high above the stage from some invisible ropes overhead. The two faces painted together on one. What were they called? He tried to remember as he filled in the mouth around his own with red.

But the kitchen drawer does not have any Japanese tea. Yokiko slides it back onto its rollers and wonders what to do. She is worried that Wan will think poorly of her and her American tea. He will think she has abandoned more than she bargained for, more than she promised when she left Japan for New York. He will think she is no longer the daughter, the sister, the nurse, she used to be. She is worried he will not know her anymore. She is afraid of that searching look she imagines he will turn on her as he tries to place the person before him.

Maggie felt a flight of worry in her chest. What would it mean if it didn't become clear by the end of the book why Marcus had been reminded of her? She let this thought pass, feeling the tenderness beneath it, as if exploring it further would mean the possibility of losing something. Six weeks was not a long time, not long enough to really know someone. She let her worry go, settling somewhere inside her, resting like a sheer scarf over a dark hole, wavering slightly to let her know it was still there. She found her place back with Yokiko turning off the kettle hissing loudly on the stove.

Yokiko moves it off the burner and checks the boxes in the back of her closet now for the right kind of tea.

Something desperate flies through her but it is too thin and amorphous to grab hold of. It moves through her like a ghost, like the wind, and makes her cold.

Samuel ran up the hallway to the terrace's screen door. He pressed his painted face against the screen and called to his mother on the terrace, thinking he'd got it.

"Mommy," he called, "What's a Siming twin?"

"What?" Her voice trailed slowly back to him inside.

"Simings twin?"

"You mean, Siamese twin?" Through the screen he could see the back of her ponytail over the low plastic chair. He could see the small black type on a corner of the page as she held up her book to shield the sun.

He pressed his face into the screen, closing one eye. "That! I'm gonna be one," he told her, pressing his hands against the screen door. The back of her ponytail swung lightly as she shook her head.

"They're born like that, Sammy," she said turning another page, "you can't become one."

"Why not?" he said. "*And* an astronaut." Samuel slid open the screen. His mother removed her sunglasses and lowered her book. Now there were two sets of eyes looking at him.

"See?" He showed off his face covered in his mother's lipstick. "With the pink like that on one eye, and the mouth..." He squiggled his finger.

"Ah, Sammy, come on, wash that off. I told you that's not for you. Don't use make-up to paint on your face like that."

His mother stood and led Samuel back through the door now stained with bits of pink and red pressed into the screen.

Samuel went into the bathroom to wash, and his mother caught a glimpse of the metal tubes lined along the mirror. A flatness expanded inside of her, and she didn't know what to do with it.

"Come out when you're done," she called after gently shutting the door and returning to the terrace.

Yokiko is adding sugar to the pot of herbal tea, hoping that if she sweetens it enough, her brother will not mind. But she still feels the worry move through her. Wan will ring twice. This is their code because there are no intercoms at Yokiko's building. He will ring two short buzzes and then walk up the narrow flight to her one-bedroom apartment. He is coming to discuss the details of how to help their father. He stopped calling him *Kabocha* on the phone. For the first time in as long as she could remember her brother was calling him *Father.* She thinks this is part of the coldness, the ghost she feels move through her.

Of course, Maggie thought, she could just ask Marcus.

The setting has changed to their sick father's farm in Japan. One of Yokiko's childhood friends who is still a nurse at the soldier base is sitting by Yokiko's father, warming his face with a washcloth while he lies in bed. She is reminiscing about Yokiko and Wan to the sick father, about how they used to play games; the game they loved most was with the berries, how they'd squish them to use the color to mark a path on which the others would get lost. A game of hide and seek plotted by berry stains. If they were found, they'd pick a whole new batch of berries to start again on another path so as not to cross new trails with the old. The friend brings the washcloth down Yokiko's father's cheek, around his chin and neck, to the back of his head which she lifts with her palm. She is a good nurse, the father wants to tell her, but part of what makes him unable to say it is the constriction in his chest and the rawness in his throat, and the other part has something to do with the fact that his own daughter is a nurse, too, but that this is not his daughter. And listening to the young nurse tell stories of her youth with his own children, after all these years, he is not sure of the girl's name. He can picture her in braids standing with his daughter, being called in for tea; he can see the girl's mother and father, the conversations they would have when coming from next door, but now on his bed where he lies being washed by the grown girl's hands, she is somebody new, and he does not know what to call her. The nurse continues, remembering her youth as she tends to the bedside of a dying man who was once her best friend's father, and together she is nurse, and woman, and a childhood girl from next door.

A bird landed on the rail of the terrace startling Samuel's mother from the page, from the feeling of coming close to understanding something. Her son was still inside. She put the book down on its open spine beside the bowl of warming cherries and left the author's face to stare up at the bright sky.

"Sammy?" she called. He didn't answer. Down the carpeted hallway, past the bathroom, the linen closet, her bedroom, to his bedroom, her eyes still adjusting to the indoor light, she stopped in his doorway. He was lying in his bed, under the sheets. Through the curtains held open by the tiny nails, the sunlight fell in one thick stripe across his covered body.

A few months ago, Samuel was lying in bed listening to his mother hammer tiny nails into his curtains, until they were pinned open to let in light. *You sleep when it's dark in here,* she'd said, *that's all, it's a beautiful day.* She kept saying, *it's a beautiful sunny day, look at how sunny and bright.* Samuel got up and thought *mama's in love with the sun.*

"Sammy?" She walked toward his bed. It was that flatness again stretching out inside her. "What's the matter?"

He was halfway dreaming. Bright painted faces marked with kisses, the round lipstick O's that stay on cheeks. So many O-marked faces calling his name, perfectly shaped letters floating through the air with all their swirls and curves.

She sat down feeling her son's back through the sheet. "Sweetheart," she whispered. "Get up."

The letters spelled his name. The sound of his name being carried away. But not by Faroozi, not by his gang. He heard his mother say his name softly.

She felt the small cradle shape of her son's head and patted his hair gently. Across the room a little gold frame sat on his dresser. It held a picture of the two of them together at the zoo. It was from a couple of years ago. Samuel had grown since then. She thought of Marcus, imagining how it would look with him standing there in that picture with them.

"Come on, baby. It's a beautiful day. We'll go do something." She rocked his shoulder.

Samuel sat up. His feet hung half-way to the ground, his soft cheek still smudged with a faint trace of red. She licked her thumb. "How about we go to the zoo?" His face contorted as she lightly rubbed his cheek.

Samuel made a fist around his thumb and then with his other hand worked to open his first and last finger. He held it up and bounced it in the air, looking for a shadow on the wall. In the corner, a little clock tat-tatted, a metal head tatting and shaking *what a shame.* He moved the rabbit to the sound of the tic across the green and white striped wallpaper. He wiggled the rabbit's ears behind the green bars of wallpaper cage. Tat, tat, tat. *Shame, shame,* Rita would say. *Shame on you, niño.* Even though that was not his name.

Maggie stared at the frame. "What do you say? Zoo sound fun?"

Samuel moved the rabbit through the green bars across his room. The shadow of his hand passed quickly across the frame as he aimed his fist around the room.

Marcus did suggest they all three do something this afternoon. She could call him. Ask him to join them. The three of them could go together. The little gold clock ticked in the corner. They could go to the zoo. It's something people did. Something people did together.

At two-thirty, they met at the front entrance by the seals. She was unusually nervous. Samuel was eating a bag of popcorn. When she had grabbed her oversized canvas tote, she tossed in the book. Now the bag hung heavy from her shoulder with the book inside. She and Marcus watched Samuel run ahead to see the lions.

"Interesting," Marcus said, stopping to read the wooden signpost. "Peafowls," he read. The ostrich-like birds wandered the edges on the lion's cage. "Never heard of them, but amazing how they live together like that, isn't it?" Marcus seemed too comfortable being with her and Samuel, like he was used to them being a family together. She watched Samuel sidestepping along the metal fence. He always seemed so lonely, and she felt responsible.

"Sammy," she called.

"Hey sport, take a look at this," Marcus called to her son. He waved him over and started to read lion facts aloud from the sign.

"I have to go to the bathroom," Samuel said.

The three of them walked to the primate house and it was dark and crowded inside. The stairs leading to the lower level where the bathrooms were located were packed with people.

"I can take him," Marcus offered.

"You sure? Thanks. Ok, Sammy, go ahead with Marcus. I'll wait outside, right in front."

She maneuvered through the crowds, past the smudged glass cages, and went outside to sit on a bench by the gorillas. The largest gorilla was sprawled on its back with a baby the size of Samuel curled against him. Another pair was picking through each other's hair. She liked looking at them. It felt reassuring, like the gorillas had figured it all out, and it was really all that simple.

She pulled the book from her bag.

Wan is tall and has to duck to enter the threshold of Yokiko's doorway. Yokiko has finished making the pot of American herbal tea with too much sugar. It lets out a thin rise of Chamomile steam. She leaves it on the stove and brings the plate of biscuits to the living room where she sits next to Wan.

Wan takes a biscuit and though he doesn't say so, Yokiko knows he is waiting for tea. "I've figured my savings," Yokiko says and gets up from the couch. She returns to the kitchen and gets a pencil and paper from the drawer. She takes the teapot and fills the two cups but leaves them on the counter. She sits down on the couch and starts to write out her calculations, avoiding his eyes. Wan watches over his sister's math, guarding with his palm the crumbs that drop as he bites his biscuit. She says, "How much will he need?" Wan is unsure. "He would never say something like that. You know it isn't his nature," he tells her. Wan has been in the United States less than a year, five years less than Yokiko, and though hers is mainly masked, Yokiko notices his accent when he uses English words. Yokiko says she knows their father wouldn't say. "It is typical," she agrees, nodding. "Just like him,"The tea in the kitchen is getting cold.

"Mama!" Samuel cried and his mother jumped. She shut the book, slipped it back into her bag.

Samuel came running towards her holding a cardboard tube up to his mouth. His knees were knobby and knocking together as he ran, cutting off a couple who stopped short. She caught the woman's eye and held up her hand in apology. They smiled and said something to each other as they walked on.

Her heart was wild.

"Mama," Samuel called through the tube covered with the sticky remains of cotton candy. He ran into her legs, and she took the tube from his mouth.

"Where'd you get this?"

"Over there." He pointed to the cement path.

"On the ground?" She wiped his mouth. "This is dirty. It's someone's garbage."

Samuel tasted a little bit of sugar leftover on his lip and watched his mother crumple his newfound megaphone between her hands.

Marcus came forward and the three of them walked along the paths together. To these strangers, she thought, they must look like a family—a mother and father and son spending a day together at the zoo. Most of that is true, she thought, searching for a trash can to throw away the wadded tube.

She glanced at Marcus who was really perfectly fine, she thought, a nice, middle-aged man who worked at an advertising firm. She felt that waver inside her again, that thin sheer scarf covering a black hole. She looked down at her son between them, his arms crossed, hands tucked inside his armpits. They continued down the path, Marcus talking about habitats, as they crossed between a young man (on her right) holding a camera to his face, and a young woman—his wife?—(on the left) waiting on the other side of the path. She heard the shutter snap and hoped maybe they'd been caught, the three of them on his film, appearing as the family she imagined they could be. Somewhere there'd be a photograph of them, and it could fit into the little gold frame in Samuel's room. But "go ahead," the man said, lowering his camera to pause as they moved past.

The book shifted in her purse, and she reached for her son's hand. He took it and squeezed. Marcus whistled and tucked his hands into his blue jean pockets, the three of them heading towards the exit, while Wan waited for his tea that Yokiko knew would never be enough.

At their building's entrance, Maggie thanked Marcus for joining them. "You can come up with us," she offered. "Lemonade if you want."

He looked at her in that genuine way he had, his dark brown eyes unafraid to hold on hers and said he would love to, but he had some work to do.

Her son was pulling her hand, stretching her arm away in the direction she wanted to go.

Marcus embraced her, and he smelled of shaving cream and mint gum, so clean, so neat, so arranged. She didn't know how he would fit with them.

He ruffled Samuel's hair. "See you, sport," he said, as Samuel pulled his mother's limp arm, yanking it backwards as though on a string, as though it no longer belonged to her.

That night from his bed, Samuel watched a pale blue robe on the back of his closet door. The empty sleeves hung loose, and in the glow of his nightlight, it looked like a ghost, but he was not afraid. A good ghost, he decided. From the window came a breeze, and it lifted her arms, dancing her slowly at first before a gust twirled her then stopped. Samuel watched the blue ghost flying but not away, dancing, lulling him to sleep, but he was no longer tired. He wanted to get up. He would go back outside. Look at the moon.

His mother was back on the terrace, reading in the dusk.

Maggie wanted Yokiko to tell Wan what she really thought, that he would lose himself here, too, if he stayed. She asks if he misses home. He says, "I do." She asks if he wants to go back. With a subtle nod, he says, "yes." Yokiko fills with a sudden urge to shout at her brother, "you can't," but she bites her lips. He says it again, and this time she says, "things will be different." But her brother doesn't seem to hear. The author explains how Yokiko remembers a childhood kite and feels herself like its golden tail flying up and away into the sky the day she lost it at the park, and that this is her Japanese blood, her connection to her dying father, and somehow in all these years away, she realizes she has lost grip of this string inside of her. Wan says, "let's have some tea." And Yokiko reflexively stands but then stops before sitting back down. "I'm sorry," she says, the two cups of herbal tea already cold in the kitchen, "I'm all out of tea," she says, because she knows to him this would be true.

The sun was a slice of orange on the horizon. Maggie didn't feel like Yokiko. She was Samuel's mother. She was a thirty-four-year-old woman who worked at a bank; she was (trying to be) a girlfriend to a thirty-eight-year-old man who lived alone; she was a daughter; an ex-wife. So many fragments of different lives swirled inside her. Yet, she felt like none of these things completely. She was a kaleidoscope of shifting selves.

The sun started to sink into the darkening sky, and she pictured the last bit of orange as the golden tail of Yokiko's kite. None of these parts had truly slipped away in her. It was Marcus who had written, *my marionette*. He had loved his puppets. And now, did he love her, too?

She shut the book on her lap and closed her eyes feeling the little bit of whatever it was she almost had with Marcus slip away. She knew she could not love him with all the many pieces that made up her heart. It hurt the same way it hurt to know the space between her and her son would keep growing.

Her son was sleeping in his room, dreaming of all the things he wanted to be. All the things he still could be. Dreaming of things he had not yet learned to name, things that when he did would fall away. He would learn which ones these were without effort or even knowing how, he would learn them like words to a song he never meant to remember. Somehow it would happen in the small unspoken ways of faces telling him yes or no, telling him right or wrong, telling him boys don't dance on moons, no one sleeps in day, telling him green is for apples, blue is for moons, you are a boy spelled S-A-M-U-E-L. She knew there was nothing she could do to stop that.

When the full moon finally rose, Samuel stood on the terrace, tracing the moon's outline with his finger. It was a perfect circle, a wide-open mouth calling *Oh*, one single hole in the solid fabric of the sky, just wide enough to crawl through. And it wobbled slightly as though it were a giant head about to fall, heavier than the sky that held it. His mother had fallen asleep in her chair, and the Asian woman lay watching from her lap. And in the little bit of moonlight across the railing, he made a spiral, then a leaf, then a small lost bird flying across the bars. And before he turned to face the wall where the light had moved, before he changed his fist to a finger so he could shadow-write his name, trying to connect each letter before it disappeared, he brought the bird down. And in this slight motion, nobody, not even Samuel, saw the shadow's sudden flight across his mother's cheek and into the stained screen where it disappeared for a second against the darkness.

A Nice Place to Retire

It was hot when they finally arrived in Jakarta. It was the furthest they'd been from home together since their honeymoon thirty years ago. This time, Ellen and Joe were here to stay. *Retire in paradise on Java's pristine shores!* Ellen had the brochure tucked into her purse; she'd carried it for the past nine months like a talisman. Their few belongings had been shipped ahead of time. Their grown son, Rock, the only thing left behind.

The welcome packets had arrived at their two-story colonial brick house in the suburbs of New Jersey. The house at 29 Riverwood Drive was no longer theirs; Joe's position as Vice President of Communications at Wiley Technologies now belonged to a kid half his age; Ellen's work at West Roger School's library would be divided among parent volunteers. Rock was twenty-nine years old and had joined a new program, sober for eight months. Life would go on.

Ellen stepped into the airport bathroom as Joe headed through the sliding doors. Outside, the air was thick with fog. Joe felt younger already, as though they'd traveled thirty years into the past. He tried to put Rock's struggles out of his mind. An entire ocean separated them now. This was a new start.

An Indonesian boy wearing dark-colored shorts took hold of Joe's suitcase, and Joe followed him toward the line of taxis crowded at the curb.

"Any of these are fine," Joe said, thanking him and pulling out his guidebook with a list of common phrases.

In the bathroom, Ellen held her hands under the sink then clapped water to her cheeks. It'd been a long flight, that's all. A second honeymoon, the realtor had called it. Easier to think of this as an extended trip. It was hard to comprehend the one-way. She tried to think of the floor plans of the condominium and the sandy beaches from the association's brochure. But of course, it was Rock who pressed into her mind instead.

He'd been Rock for most of his life, short for Richard. There was something strong and solid in him despite his thin frame, despite his drinking. Rock's new mentor had gotten him the job at Paris Blue on 43rd Street in Hell's Kitchen. It was good money. When Ellen mentioned her concern about the atmosphere, Rock brushed it aside. Joe didn't seem to have the same trouble letting go. She trusted in her husband's assuredness. The move was good for him, Joe promised. Their son needed to be on his own. He'd be fine.

The meditation app she'd been listening to on the plane resounded in her mind: *change is the only constant.* She shook off a wave of light-headedness as she stepped out through the sliding doors. The heat and fog enveloped her.

"Nice hat," Joe said, smiling as he opened the taxi's door.

"Hello, Mrs.," the driver said, motioning her inside with an open sweep of his arm. "Please."

"It's all worked out," Joe reassured her. They slid onto the cracked vinyl of the backseat, the material hot against Ellen's legs.

"Welcome," the driver said. "This is your first time here?"

"We had our honeymoon here—thirty years ago. A few days in Java and then to Bali," Joe replied.

"Very different now," the driver said. "I think you will love our country very much."

The car was suffocating. It smelled like cloves. Ellen rolled the window down and waved out an enormous silvery blue fly. Nothing looked familiar.

Joe held his Indonesian phrasebook. "It's a nice day," he attempted.

The driver replied fluently.

"Can you repeat that?" Joe said.

"Very good, sir. You wish to learn."

They sped down a busy highway, bypassing the city, and eventually the land opened up. Terraced hills spread out forever. Beneath the clouds, volcanoes rose in the distance. It seemed the entire island was surrounded in steam.

"*Borobudur*," Joe read from a flagged page.

"Of course," the driver said, keeping his eyes on the road. "Very beautiful. Very popular."

Ellen stared at the rice paddies stretching across the hills. Small villages appeared as suddenly as they disappeared.

"It says here that Jakarta was once renamed to mean Glorious Victory. Isn't that interesting?" The engine's rumble drowned out Joe's words as they bumped over dips in the road.

Ellen fanned herself as they drove deeper into the land. "Do you think our things arrived yet?"

"They said by Wednesday, so I assume everything's there."

Everything but Rock.

Two nights before they left for Java, Ellen and Joe met Rock for dinner at an Italian restaurant near his apartment in Chelsea. Joe ordered a glass of wine, and Rock, a club soda with lime.

Joe talked about the history of Indonesia. Ellen reminded Rock of their plans to fly back at least once a year, maybe more. She reminded Rock they'd pay for his ticket to visit at Christmas. Of course, they would be together for Christmas.

Joe was eating a large twist of pasta from his fork. "Flight's not bad when you have an overnight," he said. "Just one stop. You go to sleep, wake up, and you're there."

"Nothing's forever," Ellen said. "We can always come back." She reached for her son's hand and then fixed the napkin on her lap.

Rock tilted his glass back, drained the soda. "What're you gonna worry about without me, mom?"

Joe blotted his mouth. "Tell us you're going to be alright and everyone's happy."

"Send me a postcard," Rock said, leaning onto both elbows like he used to do as a kid. He shook the ice into his mouth as though unable to quench his thirst.

Ellen picked up her oversized fork and prodded her meal—a glazed chicken breast that she could not get herself to cut into, her stomach in a twist. "You'll come at Christmas. It'll be nice for you to get away at that time, I'm sure."

The waiter came with the billfold, and Ellen's heart sank. She held her hand over the check. "Wait," she said, drawing a triangle in the air between the three of them, "Shouldn't we order some dessert?" her tone more pleading than she'd intended.

She tried to focus now—the way the taxi jostled over each dip in the road, the mountains, the thick clouds streaming in. Two women wearing brightly patterned sarongs and dome shaped hats carried baskets of oranges alongside the road; a group of children—the girls in dark skirts, the boys in white shirts and red ties—carried notebooks beneath their arms. A man in the distance herded goats. A dog barked wildly. A village of thatched huts, multicolored fabrics hanging out to dry, a sculpted mosque, its metal roof shining. Ellen couldn't breathe.

"Llamas," Joe pointed.

"These are sheep," the driver said.

"Oh, Javanese sheep. They look like llamas."

Everything made her queasy as they forged deeper into the land.

Three years ago, Joe first mentioned the idea. They stood in the dark kitchen, the light above the sink cast a soft glow across the countertop which held a framed photo of Rock on his high school graduation day.

Ellen thought it sounded crazy. Joe booked a ticket to look at property. Soon after, Rock relapsed again.

The taxi slowed along a narrow ridge. A woman wearing a sarong of blue and orange swirls stuck her palm into the window. Ellen pulled her purse from the floor. The driver glanced back and shouted, flapping his hand at the window.

"I'm sorry, Miss. You do not pay."

"Oh, no. That's OK."

But the driver picked up speed.

They continued past a rocky cliff overlooking the ocean. They rounded another wide curve, descending through the fog towards the coast.

Joe read from his book. "Did I tell you this…shortly after World War II…"

It was getting hotter without air conditioning. Ellen used the association's brochure to fan herself. She knew this brochure by heart. The new construction beach homes with large glass windows faced the ocean. It was this brochure that Joe had brought home from his trip when he told her he'd found the perfect place. The brochure implied a dream come true—cerulean skies, endless beaches, views streaked with perpetual golden sunsets, and smiling children playing with a carefree abandon that children ought to have—something she never saw in Rock. It was like muscle memory, the part of her that kept reaching out for him. Her watch was still on U.S. Eastern time.

A lazy blue fly buzzed into the backseat and finally the taxi stopped. The condominiums stood scattered along the beach, awaiting their arrival.

"*Selam datang!*" A Javanese man wearing a floral-patterned shirt tucked into tan shorts waved from the complex's entrance. "Welcome!" he called, "Mr. and Mrs. Peterson."

"My name is Mr. Don," he said, pointing to the nametag on his shirt. "I believe most of your belongings arrived this morning. Please let me know if I can assist you in getting settled. You will find information inside."

"It's very exciting. Thank you so much," said Joe.

"I'm sure you will enjoy your new home."

It smelled like sawdust, free from history. The labeled boxes were set in their assigned rooms of their new two-bedroom condo. It was easier than Ellen imagined to undo an entire life. Things were not as fixed as they appeared—they could leave their jobs, sell their home, their son could live his life on his own.

"It's just like the pictures," she said.

"Same as the model," Joe nodded. "This one was being built when I came."

A vase of orchids along with a welcome note signed by Mr. Don and a copy of *The Jakarta Post*—the English language newspaper sat on the counter. A folder containing the association's policies, information on local restaurants, and a list of residents, many of whom were European and Australian as noted in parenthesis.

"I met them when I looked at the complex," Joe said, pointing at one of the names. "They've been here two years. Nice couple."

"I can't believe we're actually here." She exhaled. "Joe, I'm a wreck."

He looked up, his mouth slightly open.

"Is there something on how to make calls?" she said. "We'll need to get cell service."

"Right here." He pulled out a yellow sheet from the folder with directions on how to dial from the international calling booth.

"I'll leave Rock a message and let him know we arrived."

"Looks like it's right across the way. Behind the main building."

She hurried out, and Joe surveyed the room. He tore off a strip of tape from one of the boxes. Ellen's favorite ceramic blue mugs. He unwrapped the newspaper from one of the mugs and set it down. Maybe they shouldn't have brought anything from home. It seemed to taunt him. He shut the box and went to take a shower.

From the shower, Joe heard his wife scream. He ran, dripping, into the kitchen.

"Oh my god, look at that thing!" Ellen shouted, hands over her mouth.

He tried to wrap the condominium's bath towel around his waist.

A giant thick brown centipede stretching almost a foot long curled around the kitchen sink's basin. It looked like a small fur-covered snake with a thousand fuzzy tentacles. It appeared suctioned across the bottom of the sink.

"Damn," he said. "That's big."

"What *is* that thing?"

"I don't know. Look at all those tentacles…"

Ellen started opening boxes, hoping to find something they could use to get rid of it.

Joe stood over the sink.

Ellen looked up from where she knelt, holding the blue mug in her hand. "We need a pot."

Joe looked for a paper towel. Actually, he would need more like a shoe, but he was barefoot. He removed the small bath towel from his waist, but wasn't sure what he could do with it, how he would wrap the entire thing. What if it stung?

Various cups and bowls sat scattered around Ellen on the kitchen floor. Joe tried to refasten the towel around his waist, but the damn thing was too small. He dropped it and stood naked instead, still dripping, and considered the colander.

The centipede was too big to crush. He turned the pot upside down and carefully trapped the creature beneath. Hopefully, it would go back down the drain. But he couldn't imagine that thing could have come from there.

"We're gonna need something," he said, watching the pot. Joe picked up the towel, pulled in his gut and wrapped as tightly as he could. "It's one of the association's," he explained.

Joe thought he saw another creature slithering quickly across the floorboards, but when he looked again, it was gone. A shadow.

"Let's take a walk. Get some dinner?" he suggested. "I'll do something with this, and we'll head out."

Ellen agreed. A small flicker on the ceiling, and Ellen yelped, ducking beneath her hands. A mass of giant centipedes was crawling around the light fixture.

"I'll find Mr. Don," he said. "I'm sure he has...spray or something."

Ellen grabbed her shawl and slipped outside.

Joe found the welcome note and read Mr. Don's available hours—it was too late. They'd have to wait until morning. He found some clothes and took a careful walk through the condo. In the corner of the living room ceiling, he saw another cluster of centipedes, another in the hallway, and then another. They were nested throughout the entire condo. It was infested.

At the edge of the association's property, an outdoor restaurant overlooked the beach. The patio was filled with small tables. Large-leafed plants surrounded the borders, and colorful lit lanterns were strung above. Pop music played softly. A calling station was situated on the upper ledge of a grassy terrace.

It was Ellen's idea to call again. Back home, it was 8 a.m., and she wanted to get Rock on the phone. Joe waited at the table. He could see her through the door of the red calling station. He watched her gripping the receiver with both hands.

Joe was pouring his second glass of wine when he saw Ellen staring at him from the phone station with a strange expression. He waved her back to the table, gesturing to end the call with Rock. But she turned her back and kept talking. The waiter arrived, and Joe ordered an appetizer.

Ellen waved Joe to come take his turn on the phone. He hesitated, holding up a hand, but then, of course, hurried to the terrace.

Ellen passed him the receiver without a word.

"You there, son?" he said, watching his wife return to their table.

An overseas pause in the connection made Rock's hesitation seem too long. Joe said again, "Hello?"

"Hey, Mom says there's some nasty centipedes there."

"Well, we weren't expecting it."

Rock's laugh overlapped with Joe's voice.

When Joe had heard Ellen scream, he felt he was at home, running towards some bad news about Rock again. They could handle centipedes.

"It's actually wonderful here. We're sitting outside to eat now, looking at the ocean. Did your mother mention anything else, or just the centipedes?"

There was a screech of static. Rock's voice was mangled.

Joe said, "Everything ok?"

"What? I heard you say 'the fish' and that was it."

"I said, how are you? That's all I said."

"I'm fine. Cool as a cucumber. They have those over there?"

"Have what?"

"Cucumbers." Rock's laugh interrupted Joe's words.

"Do they have cucumbers? Is that what you are asking?"

"This is weird, right? It's like echoing. Hello, hello!"

Rock's words were sliding into one another with that familiar slant. It was only eight in the morning over there.

"I got one for you. Wait till you hear this one, Dad."

Joe waited out the pause.

"I was serving the other night, right? And guess who comes in. Brenna Roberts. Or wait, Rogers? Anyway, Brenna—from your office? Big hair, big jewelry. She was with a dude. Big dude—looked like a wrestler."

Joe felt the blood rush from his face. He looked through the glass door at Ellen talking to the waiter. He wanted to hang up. How could his mistakes follow him to the other side of the world?

"Listen, we should wrap it up," Joe tried to interrupt. But the connection was already breaking it up for them.

"But they tipped real good, or I guess the big dude did. And anyway, Dad, you might think I'm a jerk-off, but I know some things. About Ms. Brenna. You and Brenna...what five, six years ago?"

"What the hell are you doing, Richard?"

"But who am I to judge, right?"

A burst of static. He didn't want to remember the three-month affair with the administrative assistant from his office.

"You guys are happy now though, right? All the way over there in Shangri-La?"

"Listen now..."

Rock laughed.

"You probably blame it on me. Right, Dad? All the shit I put you guys through?"

"It's time to hang up now, son. We'll try to talk tomorrow. This is not the time...I can hear from your voice."

"Hey, that's all bullshit anyway. I wanted to tell you I won't make it for Christmas. Holiday season is good business, and they want me for head waiter. I know mom really wanted me to come, but if you could tell her."

It was a lie. For all Joe knew, Rock had lost his job. "Your mother will call you tomorrow. It's been a long day. We're pretty hungry."

"That you are."

"We'll talk again tomorrow."

"I'm pretty hungry myself."

"Goodbye, son."

Ellen lifted her wine glass for a toast when Joe returned to the table.

"He sounded good, don't you think? Did he tell you about his promotion?"

Joe lifted his glass to hers. "Let's enjoy our first evening." He tried to keep from sliding into regret.

Joe navigated the conversation away from Rock or the centipedes. They enjoyed their fish, fed each other a taste of this and that from their forks, hints of curry and coconut oil, spicy chili peppers, mango and pineapple. As the sun went down, the lanterns shone above the patio.

Ellen's sandals dangled from her fingers, and Joe rolled up the bottom of his slacks as they walked back along the beach. Joe reached for Ellen's waist.

"It's been so long," Ellen said, resting her cheek against Joe's shoulder.

They leaned together for a kiss, slowly exploring the forgotten territory of one another. The sand under their feet rose in uneven mounds, they were light from alcohol, a hint of fish and curry leftover in their mouths. It *was* like their honeymoon, Ellen thought as she kissed her husband, remembering how excited they were when they found out she was pregnant. She remembered the surprising colic, the way her son seemed to struggle even as an infant, the way sometimes she'd be frightened by the intensity with which he nursed in the middle of the night, his little hands gripping onto her for dear life. She felt her husband moving his fingers under the back of her hair. She thought of Rock, the man he'd grown into, finding him slouched against their front steps two years ago. Their last dinner, chewing his ice, bouncing his knee, scanning the room for the nearest exit. He was not OK.

Joe couldn't remember kissing his wife like this for years. But the image of Brenna Richards haunted him and filled him with sickening dread.

Ellen felt Joe's hands pause on her shoulders. She stepped back. "You don't believe him, do you?" she said. "About the promotion?"

The evening air was cooling. Ellen wrapped the shawl around herself.

Joe shook his head sadly.

She took a deep breath. "There was something else."

He felt the weight of Brenna Rogers wrapping a heavy leg around him, smothering him with guilt, with his own failures.

"Rock said something," Ellen said, looking out at the wide expanse of ocean. "It didn't make sense. But I have to ask."

Joe covered his face.

"Oh god," she whispered.

"I'm so sorry," he said.

"Wait." She tightened her shawl. "I thought I did, but I don't want to know."

Joe crouched down.

"I wasn't perfect either," Ellen said.

"What?"

Ellen squatted beside him. "It's all so far away now."

"What happened?"

"Can't we just leave it behind? Over there— across this ocean?"

She cupped a handful of sand.

He didn't recognize the assurance in her voice. He had no idea she ever cheated. There was a brief time when she was working with a new consultant for the school, around the same time as his affair with Brenna, that he had a slight suspicion. But in a strange way it now made him think that they'd been more connected in their isolation than either of them had realized.

A jellyfish washed up on the shore, its translucent tentacles barely visible on the wet sand. Green slashes of seaweed wrapped around its body.

"We're here now. That's for sure," Joe said. He took her hand. It was too dark to see the water. A cool breeze came off the shore.

At the stone path leading up toward the condominiums, they stopped. For so many years, Joe had tried to protect Ellen from the truth—about his affair, about Rock stealing, about how he knew Ellen gave Rock money. He needed to be honest now. "I know about the savings," he said.

"Oh, Joe." Ellen shook her head.

"I get it," he said. "You were trying to help him."

"It didn't work," she said.

"That's why I pulled the rest out. We were going to have nothing."

Ellen covered her mouth. He could see her understanding turning to tears.

"It's a good investment," Joe said, pointing at their new home.

Ellen nodded.

"He not coming for Christmas," Joe told her.

"It's still a ways off. He might."

Joe shook his head. "Let's not do this."

She knew it was true, Rock wouldn't come.

The narrow section of beach in front of the condominiums was populated with couples. It had the feel of a private cove, undiscoverable to the rest of the world, where people came to escape, to recreate themselves. They faced their new home. Ellen imagined they were observing a window display at Christmastime, some idealistic scene which, if one could just move through the glass, would become real.

Joe had left on the lights inside their condo, hoping the centipedes might find their way back outside.

"There were more," Joe said, "throughout the place."

"What do you mean?"

"A lot of those…creatures."

"What?" Ellen cried. "How many?"

"I'll find Mr. Don first thing in the morning. Don't worry."

The sky was bursting with stars.

"It's infested?"

"It's solvable."

He wanted to assure Ellen that everything would be fine—Rock, their lost savings, their marriage. He wanted to say something about the bugs, their son, the chronic disappointment—how all of that made this *real.* But he couldn't find the words. Instead he said, "It might come with the territory. We'll just have to deal with it."

Something frantic unleashed in Ellen's expression. The light reflected off her eyes, shrinking her pupils. "Isn't that what we've been doing all this time?"

He felt the ground tilt in the way it did when things began to slide out of control. An overwhelming desire fell over him to go home, back to their real home on Riverside Drive, back to their life, no matter how messy. He tried to think of something to say to make it better, something about the centipedes, about their dream coming true.

"I just need a few minutes alone out here," Ellen said.

"Please, we can face it together."

"Go. I'll be right in."

Joe hesitated. "Don't be too long."

Ellen sat on the beach. The ocean crashed loudly. That Rock's illness was her fault, that she'd failed him, that they'd never find their way back, these were the fears that wedged themselves into the ventricles of her heart, causing constrictions with every inhale. She tried to think of something from her meditation app, but everything felt like the sand sifting through her fingers.

Ellen could discern a couple laying on the sand; the shape of their embrace made them blend into one figure. She couldn't remember the last time she'd been with her husband, just the two of them without the worry of Rock between them. Maybe Joe was right, they'd flown across the world to get away, to start over. She dusted the sand off her palms.

When Joe entered the condo, the centipedes were everywhere. "Get," he hissed. He picked up the towel he'd dropped earlier and swiped at a cluster of them. But they clung to the corners and the walls, their tentacles undulating. He doubted for a moment if this was actually solvable. Maybe it was something they would have to accept as part of their new environment. He turned off the lights. Maybe in the dark, the creatures would hide. He tiptoed down the hall. In the bedroom, he opened a cardboard box and pulled out a blanket—the lime green one they'd had on their bed for years. He crawled onto the bare mattress, draping the familiar blanket over him. The floor lamp cast a circle of light on the ceiling.

Ellen felt her way inside. In the kitchen, she saw multiple overturned pots. Those things were not going to make them run away. They were here to stay, with or without them. She picked up a tennis racket from an opened box and pushed at a cluster of centipedes on the countertop. They were heavier than she imagined. They didn't budge. She used both hands and stretched the racket, giving them another shove. "Ugh," she said, "what *are* you?" The cluster uncurled itself and slithered over the edge of the counter. She left the racket and hurried down the hall.

Joe looked at Ellen in the lamp light. She looked limp and worn, as though she'd been washed in from the ocean. She came toward the bed.

"Just like home," she said, crawling onto the mattress beneath the lime blanket.

And even though it wasn't anything like home, something about their unsteadiness, the unexpectedness of what was to come, the infiltration of these unwanted arthropods, felt familiar to Joe. He thought if he opened his mouth, a tsunami might come pouring out.

Ellen brought her head to rest on his chest.

"I'm so sorry," his voice cracked.

Ellen sat up. "Joe?"

But it was too much. He couldn't bear to tell her that he was wrong, that he couldn't help their son, or that no matter how far they went, it would never be enough, that the distance wouldn't change a thing. An ocean couldn't separate them from the worry they'd always feel. He was sorry he'd brought them across the world to these centipedes. It was proof—the trouble will always follow. He couldn't protect them from it.

The waves whipped violently through him. Yet his wife of thirty years held him now, strong enough for both. He felt her arms across his back, anchoring him.

"Everything's going to be fine," she said, and for the first time in as long as she could remember, she believed it. Something about those centipedes made her certain. It felt good to say. She said it again.

They lay together beneath the lime green blanket. Joe held onto her like a buoy.

The room was empty aside from their unpacked boxes. Ellen listened to Joe's breathing settle into the low steady rhythm of sleep. She rolled onto her back and saw another centipede, the biggest one yet, creeping into the circle of light on the ceiling. Its long thick body stretched above her, waving its furry tentacles. She considered turning off the lamp, but she wanted to see where it was going.

The centipede stopped at the edge of the light. Ellen waited for the creature to keep moving. It slowly slithered across the ceiling, all the way to the edge where the ceiling met the wall and stretched its body along the seam.

Joe snored softly, and she moved closer beside him, comforted by his familiar scent. Tomorrow, they would unpack. They would get some furniture—a desk, nightstands, something for the walls. Yes, tomorrow they would settle in. They would start to make it a real home. A dresser over there. A mirror over here. Linens, maybe even a canopy for the bed. She'd always wanted a canopy. Something with islets or lace.

The centipede inched along the crevice of the wall, making its silent stitch around the room. She watched its smooth, precise movements, mending their walls, securing them safely inside.

Tomorrow, she thought, tomorrow she and Joe would go to the markets.

Commedia dell'Arte

It was a cliché, really and this is what bothered Barbara the most. Here she was, almost forty, sitting on their living room carpet, in this house, in this life, searching for signs—she could've been a *Redbook* article, right here in her living room with its Shaker Beige walls and Alabaster trim. She pulled a shirt from her husband's suitcase still packed from the business trip he'd returned from last night and searched the collar for lipstick stains. It was ridiculous. Bill would never have an affair. But it was Dr. Hertz who had suggested it. She was *checking things out,* as he'd put it at her and Bill's last therapy session six months ago. It was during this session that they'd come to terms with the fact that they would not try for another baby, that they'd raise Maddy as an only child.

Dust particles clustered in the air. The sun shone through the bay window. She discerned a faint smell—she couldn't place it—something like powder and carpet cleaner, of stillness and being alone. The smell was barely discernable, but it was there. Was this the smell that other people identified as *Barbara and Bill's house*? It never dawned on her before. House smells didn't linger—it wasn't as though later that night when you hung up your clothes, there was still that hint of cinnamon from Jackie's, or that musty old book smell from Rob and Karen's, or that lemony laundry smell—Andrew and Rita's. But here it was. Barbara and Bill's. Was it possible to change it? She didn't think so. Even if she tried for the lemony laundry, or the wintergreen candles, their house would have their scent. It was the combination of what people emitted together. She wondered if Randy's changed after Joanne moved out. She wondered what hers would be if she lived alone—something like fennel or lavender, maybe, but probably some variation of powder, vacuum.

At half past six, when Bill appeared in the kitchen, he had already changed into his sweatpants.

"I heard the garage," Barbara said, pulling the lasagna out of the oven.

"Why are there so many half-eaten yogurts in here?" Bill said inside the refrigerator.

A chill from the open door moved up her neck.

He opened a bottle of Miller Light. "Randy's back."

"Really? Ouch." She grabbed the dishrag, letting the cold water run over a small burn on her thumb. A moon-shaped welt appeared on her skin.

"Yep, Joanne came home. They're back together."

"You're kidding." She shut the water. "How does that work?"

Bill shrugged.

"Some people," she said, wrapping the cool rag around her thumb.

Dr. Hertz's office was in an old loft building beside the train tracks. They'd never been to a marriage counselor before, but since Randy's split with Joanne, he'd been talking about Dr. Hertz, telling Bill that he and Joanne were having a great time at the sessions. That's what he said, *a great time.* Bill told Barbara, and they'd agreed to give it a try. Maybe it would be good to talk about the miscarriages. They drove in their own cars and met each other there after work.

Midway through their final session, Dr. Hertz stood up and printed the word *connection* in capital letters on a large pad of paper propped on an easel beside his chair. The fumes from the red permanent marker filled the space. Dr. Hertz explained that he often chose a word he felt best addressed the issue needing nurturing. They sat in a circle of five folding chairs, leaving the two beside Dr. Hertz empty. The glass coffee table against the exposed brick wall held a Hertz rental car mug stuffed with individually wrapped candies. A plastic dispenser contained lavender-colored brochures—*Discovering Divorce* scripted in elegant black font.

"Connection," Dr. Hertz said, tapping the easel, "is key." He told them it was important to check in with one another like you would a boss or a co-worker. "Size it up," he said. "Measure the love. Think of it like a child you must care for, like you are taking its temperature, your marriage's temperature. Or weighing produce at the grocery store." Barbara was annoyed; he was mixing his metaphors. He searched for another as he sat back down. "Find out if each of you are still in the game, so to speak."

Dr. Hertz seemed too tall for his folding chair and his thick glasses enlarged his eyes.

"So, how exactly do you take your marriage's temperature?" Dr. Hertz said rhetorically. Barbara knew her marriage's temperature already—not hypothermic, rather just hovering beneath the normal mark.

Bill crossed his ankle over his knee and was scratching the bone under his sock. She wasn't sure what they were doing here. Neither of them wanted to explore the weakness in their foundation. Pull one string and the whole piñata tumbles down.

"Well, for one," Dr. Hertz said, answering himself, "you can look for things. For instance, how the other greets you…or you can check each other out when you're making love…or look for things. Like lipstick on the collar." He took his large index finger and drew it along his own shirt collar.

Barbara laughed, bemused by the suggestion. They were far too settled for something like that.

As soon as Barbara had opened the suitcase, she felt ridiculous. *Who wears lipstick anymore?* But still the arousal of nerves squirreled inside her. Was it the thought that Bill might come home and catch her snooping, or was it the possibility that she might actually find something, a bit of pink pressed onto his collar? She pulled her husband's brown checkered shirt that she'd bought him last year for Christmas onto her lap. She envisioned a scene from a movie. Bill would never stray. Even Bill's secretary, Ilene, who Barbara had wondered about years ago, eventually revealed her interest in Randy. She tried to imagine the sort of woman Bill might be attracted to—someone assertive, fashioned in business suits and pumps. A pang of jealousy struck her, lighting her up like a bulb.

The automatic sprinkler turned on in the front yard, spraying scats of water across the windows. The September sun lingered in the early evening sky.

"What happened to your hand, Mom?" Maddy bounded in, slinging her book bag on the stairs, and collapsing into her chair at the dinner table. She guzzled down the glass of milk, elbows propped on the table, her light brown hair pulled back into a ponytail.

"Just a mild burn," Barbara said, serving her daughter a giant heap of lasagna. "How was play practice?"

"Good," Maddy said, her mouth already stuffed. She recounted last night's story of Jenny Brooks who was still mad at Kristy because she got to be one of the Pick-a-little Ladies even though it was obvious, she was *much* better, and even though Jenny Brooks and Maddy were cast as the townspeople's kids, the *only* difference being Kristy sang *one* extra song, it was really the same as the chorus anyways so whatever, she shouldn't be so mad, and anyway, she said shoving more lasagna into her mouth, "you should've seen it, Brad was all over Kristy. It was gross. Mrs. Oscar had to separate them. Whatever, she was totally asking for it. Can I have some more milk?"

"Chew your food."

"Before I forget," Bill said. "Randy and Joanne want to have dinner Thursday night. Over at Picardinos."

"Can I eat at Katy's?" Maddy asked.

"Picardinos? What happened to Verns? They always want to go to Verns. Or at least used to."

"Can I, Mom?"

"Sure, that's fine. I'll just check with Katy's mom."

Bill shrugged. "Guess they want do to something different."

"That's fine." She cut her lasagna. "We'll get fancy."

"Ugh, I've got homework," Maddy said.

"Go ahead." Barbara stood to clear. Maddy grabbed her backpack and skipped the stairs, singing, "Seventy-Six Trombones."

Since Dr. Hertz, they'd never again talked about the miscarriages. Just once, Barbara thought it would come up. She was carrying a basket of dirty laundry down the stairs as Bill was heading up. They stopped, facing one another on the steps, the large plastic basket between them. Bill looked at the dirty clothes. He reached into the pile and drew up one of Maddy's gym socks turned inside out, letting it dangle for a moment. Then he dropped it back in and continued up the stairs. She stared at it like it was a dead rodent, something bearing the burden between them, something irreparable. Her fault. She felt a tiny box slam shut inside her and lock.

Through their bedroom wall, she heard Maddy singing, "Till There Was You," which Maddy couldn't believe was a Beatles song because she only knew it from her play.

"I don't get it," Barbara said when Bill started talking again about Joanne and Randy.

"She told Randy she was tired. That's what she told him when she came back."

"Tired?" Barbara said. She set down her face cream without opening it.

Bill removed the mound of pillows neatly arranged on their king-sized bed. Two overstuffed rectangles, four tasseled squares, three dark red circles, two small rolls. Eleven utterly useless pillows.

"Who *isn't* tired?" Barbara said, watching him.

"That's what Randy said."

At work on Monday, the Axis memo announced the arrival of an Inspiration Coach, Dr. Pierre Vardo, for a week-long initiative to improve employee motivation. The first meeting was scheduled at ten o'clock today.

A box of munchkins sat unopened in the break room. Life affirming quotations were tacked to the bulletin board beside the CPR poster and instructions on how to fix a paper jam. Xeroxed fliers with Dr. Pierre Vardo's credentials and quoted reviews had been set on the table. Barbara read some: *We have a new sense of unity in the office and sales have increased by ten percent. Dr. Vardo has rejuvenated our corporate environment. His compassionate method worked wonders on the general morale of our company. Dr. V has healed our corporate family. Pierre is a miracle worker.*

Anne was arranging chairs in a circle when Barbara arrived in the conference room. The table had been removed at the request of the Inspiration Coach.

Barbara brought some papers to work on before the meeting began. She used her new reading glasses hanging from the brown cord around her neck that she'd bought the other day from CVS. This was one of the things that made her feel old. She began editing when Haley, the new designer hurried in and sat down.

"Thought I was late," Haley said, full of energy as usual. Haley recently graduated from Boston University and had moved to Chicago a few months ago with her boyfriend who was in a band.

Rich, of course was already there; Sampson, the programmer, arrived next, and Jerry materialized in his quiet way without anyone seeing him having entered.

When the speaker arrived the ventilation system kicked on. "I hope everybody is doing well. Good Morning." He introduced himself as Pierre.

He stood in the center of the room. Barbara guessed he was in his mid-forties. He wore a dark suit with a red printed tie. His thick hair was pulled back into a small ponytail, but a few unruly curls spilled out and hung loosely around his handsome face. His features were sculpted with a kind of generous imperfection—wide-set eyes curving downwards, a globular nose, and full lips surrounded by stubble that hinted at having arose just moments before. He looked uncontainable, like he was pushing the very edges of himself.

The word *tired* flashed into Barbara's mind. She wondered what word Dr. Hertz might have written for Randy and Joanne on that pad of paper. She imagined them sitting in his circle of chairs *having a great time.*

Pierre Vardo did not look tired.

He was wearing a ring, but it was not a wedding band. It was on the opposite hand, and he wore it on the middle finger. It was large and made of a dark metal and had some kind of three-dimensional design carved into the top—an animal head or a face.

"Thank you so very much for inviting me here." Pierre Vardo commanded the attention of the room. "I imagine and hope today will be illuminating for you." He had a slight accent and Barbara wondered where he was from.

The activity was supposed to create better listening and coping skills, a closer union in their office, easier communication and greater efficiency. He asked for a volunteer.

Rich tapped his pen lightly against his lap. Barbara held still, conscious of her eyeglasses hanging from that ridiculous cord around her gray sweater. She felt like a schoolgirl and thought of Maddy. One of the hardest things was sitting back to witness the familiar territory into which her daughter would tread for the first time—the boys, the friends. It was like watching a play you had seen before and knowing there was nothing you could do to change the outcome, nothing you could do to redirect the actors on stage. But she also knew it was part of growing up, and all she could do was be there when Maddy found the love of her adolescent life, and then again when she came home crying, crossing out the boy's name written in scattered hearts all over her notebook.

Haley nudged Barbara. "I think he wants *you*," she whispered. Barbara saw the speaker extending his hand. Before she could protest, he was leading her into the center of the room.

She folded her arms around her midsection. Why in the world did Rich have to waste their time with this kind of thing.

"Now, the objective," Pierre said to the room, then motioned for her to uncross her arms, "is receptivity."

He smiled and tucked a stray hair behind his ear.

Up close, she noticed the design on Pierre Vardo's red tie was an array of miniature gray whales. They were scattered without any particular order, designed to look as though they were swimming, each one angled in a different position. It made her dizzy.

"You are not to touch each other's palms, but to be close enough where you can feel the energy coming from one another. You can anticipate how your partner will move."

He held up his hands. The silver ring on his middle finger looked like a dragon head with wings, a fierce toothy mouth with a flame.

"You want to trace one another's movements. Follow the lead. Each will take turns leading so you can both experience the receptivity, the state of openness."

He held his palms up to face Barbara and instructed her to do the same. "When I move my hands," Pierre Vardo said to the room, "I'm sorry—" his eyes traveled down the entire length of her, "—what is your name?"

She told him and when he repeated, it sounded exotic in a way it never had before. It was a new name. "Bar-ba-ra." He pronounced the middle syllable. Made three syllables out of what her entire life had been a two-syllable name.

"I will move my hands, and Bar-ba-ra will follow," Pierre explained.

She could smell cigarettes on his breath, and it surprised her how good it smelled.

"You will look into your partner's eyes, but do not intimate which direction you will go. No. It is to be felt. Expressed and received." His large palms were facing hers, and he began moving them slowly through the space between them.

Barbara concentrated on his hands, slowly following them up, then right, left, and down, mirroring him. She felt her glasses swaying from their cord with her movements, and she wanted to sit down.

"Very good," he said to Barbara. She could feel him staring at her, but she avoided his gaze, looking off somewhere past his shoulder. "Keep going." The pin on the lapel of his jacket matched the dark silver of his ring, but it was a mask—the kind worn in a masquerade.

"And as you move with your partner, you will feel warmth build up between your hands." He slowly slid one of his palms upwards, and Barbara lifted her own to follow. "Very nice," he said, and when he smiled, a heat flooded her, and she felt one of those whales swimming in her belly.

"In essence, you are opening yourself to a receptive state, one which leaves behind your intentions, your expectations, your judgments, and this is the same feeling you want to remember when you are listening to your clients, your coworkers."

Their hands were inches apart. It was true, whatever he had just said about the warmth.

He recommended doing this exercise with a coworker at the start of the day *to tune your inner receptors*, he said. *To remind yourself of possibility.*

"It is very important." He spoke beyond Barbara while she focused on their palms moving. She had no idea the last time she stood this close to Bill. "Receptivity is the key to connection. You must receive as well as initiate, just as we are doing here. Bar-ba-ra and I."

Barbara and I. She felt like she was getting better at anticipating his direction. She liked receiving. She liked the smell of cigarettes, and the movement of those tiny gray whales across his red tie, and the silver mask on his lapel. His palms stopped, and he wrapped his hands briefly around hers, brought them together in his clasp and then bowed slightly before letting go. Her fingers curled into two loose fists by her side, and she flushed.

Rich was taking notes. Jerry was clapping softly. Sampson was asleep. Haley was discreetly texting on her phone, and Anne was stifling a yawn behind her palm. Pierre extended his arm towards her seat, releasing her.

Later that evening, when Bill was reading the paper and softly whistling the refrain from "Seventy-Six Trombones," Barbara sat down, mindlessly flipped open a magazine, and noticed Bill's familiar hands—his long, lanky fingers, the bony knuckles.

He glanced up. "What's up?"

"Oh. Nothing." She brushed the air.

Back to the paper. Whistling. The song was in her head now.

"I'm gonna head up early." What could she say? She was worn out from *tuning into her inner receptors*? That she was *tired?*

"Night," she said and marched up the stairs to Pierre's refrains—*to remind yourself of possibilities...of all the infinite connections that are possible in the course of one day...so often missed...*

The next day Barbara ran into Pierre Vardo smoking outside the building. "Barbara," he said, exhaling a long stream of smoke. Yes, Bar-ba-ra. She wanted a cigarette.

Inside the building's cafeteria, Pierre joined her at a table.

"What is that?" She pointed to the silver mask pinned to the lapel of his jacket. She resisted the instinct to pull on her glasses and lean closer.

"Do you know Commedia dell'arte?"

Barbara peeled the damp plastic off the sandwich and told him she didn't.

Pierre swirled his coffee. "Do you like the theater?"

"Sure," she said. She had a mouth full of sandwich and grabbed a napkin. "I don't know much about it, but I have a daughter and she's in her school play. She loves it."

I have a daughter. She hated the way she sounded. *You never talk in the plural. This happened to us, didn't it? No. Was it* our *body?* Even Dr. Hertz had been out of his territory then.

"That is wonderful," Pierre said. "Many children love Commedia dell'arte."

The cover of a playbill to a show that she and Bill had seen years ago popped into her mind. The image matched his pin. "Wait, I think I *have* seen it once."

"Yes?" His thick eyebrows arched upwards.

"It was a small theater. Everyone was sitting cramped together—that's what I remember. Is that funny? To remember how we were sitting? I can't even tell you what the play was about."

And that they were late. The usher with his tiny light guiding the way. Maddy at home with a babysitter. A night out together. Something to connect them for an hour or two, Dr. Hertz had suggested.

"That is very good for Commedia."

"What is?"

"That closeness to the audience."

"Oh. You would have liked this place then."

"It is about the four human emotions."

Barbara laughed, surprising herself. "Four?"

"Well. It is in the interest of study."

He folded down his first finger. "We have Joy," he said.

Barbara took a drink from her water bottle.

"Anger," Pierre continued, folding the second finger.

All she could think of was that Joanne's entire reason for leaving her family was because she was tired. But she was pretty sure Pierre wasn't going to mention that one. Was that even an emotion?

"Sorrow," he said.

"And last of all, fear." He said it gently as if setting the word carefully on the table.

It felt dangerous to continue the conversation. She pulled the plastic wrap over the half of her tuna sandwich and balled it for the trash. She glanced at the cafeteria's clock. Forty minutes had passed. "I have to get back," she said.

Picardinos was bustling for a Thursday night. Barbara sat at a corner table with Randy and Joanne. Bill was running late.

"Let's order some wine," Randy decided, then shot his hand in the air, half standing in his seat. Barbara saw Bill weaving his way through the crowded tables.

"Hi everyone," he said, pulling off his leather gloves. He shook Randy's hand and gave Joanne a sideways hug. "Traffic was a mess. It was backed up by the exit all the way to Central." Bill came around the table, leaned down to kiss Barbara's cheek.

"What'd you take—'90?" Randy said.

"Yeah."

"It was clear when we got on," Randy said. "Probably an accident."

Bill assessed the table to see what had occurred. "Wine? Did you order yet?"

"We were just about to," Randy said.

"Good evening," the waiter appeared and began with the specials.

Barbara could smell the cold air and stale office on Bill. He perched his reading glasses on his nose and examined the wine menu while Randy and Joanne ordered appetizers. He held up the menu and told him to bring a bottle for the table. His shirt sleeves were rolled up and as he loosened his tie, Barbara drew her gaze around his collar. What did she think she'd see? A bright pink stain of lipstick from a kiss? She felt pathetic.

Joanne looked great. She wanted to ask Joanne what happened? Did she just wake up one day and pack her things? Did she cook dinner for herself? Did she clean or just let things go? Did she notice anything different? A new smell?

The three of them were laughing at something. Barbara had missed it. Joanne stroked the back of Randy's head. Bill reached for butter to spread on his bread.

"It seems like you're really happy," Barbara said, leaning in towards Joanne across the table.

"Thanks." Joanne glanced towards Randy, and he took hold of her hand.

Bill placed his arm around Barbara's seatback.

Joanne hummed. Or glowed. "It feels…new. I mean, I never thought—"

"What does?" Randy said. The men had tuned in.

"I was telling Barbara how much better things are."

"You know what it was?" Randy said. "It was that Dr. Hertz. He had the greatest idea. Told us to get out. Plan dates. *Without* the kids. It's so simple. But great. Really."

Barbara chided herself for searching Bill's collar. What kind of advice was that?

"And with two kids," Bill said. "I mean that's impressive." He tore off a piece of the steaming loaf. "We hardly get out, and we only have one."

Barbara felt the sting.

"Is someone smoking?" Joanne said, looking offended as she glanced around the restaurant.

Randy frowned. "Where?"

Barbara noticed Joanne's hand flutter to her belly as she searched for the source of smoke.

It must have been early yet. Not even three months. Her wine sat untouched beside the tall glass of Seven-Up. Or course. It was suddenly clear. That glowing secret.

"Over there at the bar," Bill said. And they all looked. Sure enough, at the very end of the bar, all the way across the other side of the room, an elderly man sitting alone was smoking.

Some intolerable heat flashed through her. Where in the world did this feeling fit within the four human emotions? She thought of asking Pierre Vardo. *Sorrow,* she decided, but maybe it was *fear.* Just then the salads arrived, the waiter with his mill offering pepper, and Barbara excused herself to go to the restroom.

The next day, Barbara sat in Pierre's black sports car as the two of them drove to the Bistro Grill for lunch. It was Friday—his last day at Axis and things had livened up in their office that week. She even saw Jerry and Sampson trying the palm tracing game one afternoon in the break room. Pierre had stopped by her desk and invited her, or rather explained he had a reservation at one o'clock., and he wanted to treat her to lunch for being his volunteer the first day, as a thank you. She hesitated, and Pierre, cool and calm, told her to meet him at the elevators in ten minutes, and promised it'd be fun. She slid her cold sandwich back into her bag and agreed.

The bistro was a few miles from the office—the closest restaurant beyond Ruby Tuesdays, which would be jammed at this time of day. Only a few other diners were seated at the narrow tables covered with shiny glasses and white tablecloths beneath the massive domed ceilings and dim lighting.

Pierre ordered Pernod. Barbara resisted, knowing she still had a pile on her desk to get through before the end of the day and ordered a Diet Coke.

She leaned across the table into the lighter Pierre held. He flicked it, and she pulled on the cigarette perched between her dry lips. The flame caught the tip of the barrel, and she allowed herself one slow drag and then removed it from her lips, handing the cigarette back across the table to Pierre.

"Oh God." She coughed once and laughed. "Thank you for letting me do that. It's been about twenty years since I've had one."

He slid the pack of cigarettes from his shirt pocket. "You are welcome, of course."

"No, no." She laughed again. "I don't smoke."

Pierre watched her curiously. He slid the pack back into his pocket. The waiter brought their drinks, but she wanted the cigarette taste to linger a little longer.

"You were telling me about your daughter's interest in the theater," he said, taking a sip of his drink.

"*Music Man*," she told him. "It's the first time the school has let the fourth graders try out."

"And she enjoys it?"

"She really does." Barbara nodded deeply, tasting her bottom lip. She thought of Maddy happily singing and realized she really was OK. *Plenty of only children are just fine.*

"Every night, I have the songs in my head," Barbara said. "She goes around singing all the time."

Let's go back to the two of you together. You seem hurt. Would you say you are angry?

"Young people experiencing the opportunity for transformation. It is so important," Pierre said. "The stage can be a magical place. A relief from…the stickiness of adolescence."

She'd never thought of it that way. She imagined what they looked like sitting there under the painted ceiling, scattered clouds on its domed ceiling, a couple under a faux blue sky.

"And does she have young love?" Pierre said. "Maybe that is a challenge for you." Pierre's shirt stretched over his broad shoulders, the slate-gray color bringing out some gold flecks in his dark eyes.

She picked up her soda. "No, nothing like that yet," she said. She wanted to take Maddy out of the discussion, keep it professional. "So, do you think you've helped us over there? At Axis?" she said.

Pierre's eyes settled on her. "I don't know. What about you?" he said. "Do you think I've helped you?"

A pod of those miniature whales swam around her stomach. Her right palm began to sweat, and she rubbed it on the napkin covering her lap. She thought she might cry.

"Yes?" he asked, watching her, his forearms perched on the table, fingertips pressed together making a cage of empty space.

She never imagined dinner. It was Saturday night; Bill was out of town on business, and Maddy was having a sleepover. Barbara pulled slowly into the parking lot of Ciao Bello on the north side of the city. She shut off the ignition and sat for a moment in the dark, pulling up her strapless shift dress, telling herself it was just dinner with a colleague. She hurried into the restaurant's oversized doors, bracing herself against the cold.

Pierre was waiting inside the foyer. The restaurant was dark, and the tables were lit with candles. The host greeted them in a low voice, inviting them to follow, and Pierre placed his hand on her lower back, guiding her gently ahead of him toward a small private table by a window.

The host was pulling out her chair, and a thin paper menu was in her hands, and a waiter was describing specials. Pierre kept his eyes fastened on her.

Champagne, and two flutes filled, a napkin folded over the waiter's arm.

Barbara pulled her silk scarf around her shoulders.

Pierre was lifting his glass in a toast.

The word affair hadn't entered her mind. Or maybe, she'd fought to keep the word out.

Jazz played softly from the restaurant's speakers. She recognized the tune. A swanky rendition of "Till There Was You."

"I am very happy you joined me tonight." Pierre held his glass mid-air.

Why was she so cold?

"What do you think right now, Bar-ba-ra?"

Of all the songs. She pictured Maddy on stage, wrapped in her bustier dress with its billowing skirt, marching along with the chorus as the music man deceived the townspeople. But didn't he end up charming them in the end? If she remembered correctly, wasn't it a happy ending?

How did she end up here?

"Pierre," she said directly. "I'm married."

He nodded, his face open, receptive. "Yes," he said. "I imagine you are many things."

His answer surprised her.

"We are more than our titles, yes?" he said.

Her mouth felt like sand.

"What do you think, *Bar-ba-ra*?" Pierre said. He slid his hand across the table, palm up.

What did she think?

She gripped her cold fingers on her lap.

You don't feel what I feel. It didn't happen to you. It happened to us. No. It didn't.

She knew her husband would never forgive her.

Pierre gently prodded, "What do you think?"

She thought it was possible she was no longer in love with the man she had married. But wasn't love more complicated than just being in or out of it?

She thought there must be more than four categories of emotions.

She thought she should go home, to her and Bill's home, where she belonged.

She wondered if anyone knew how tired she was?

She thought to tell Pierre how tired she was.

She picked up her champagne glass and brought it to her lips. Pierre did the same. He was following her lead now. She took a full bubbly sip. He did the same.

The music played, all swagger and pitch.

It happened to us.

Then everything seemed to stop at once, filling her with a strange wild urge.

She stared at her glass.

Her dark red lips stained the rim, a print pressed in Maybelline's *Pearled Plum* that she had bought from CVS on her way here tonight.

She couldn't take her eyes off it. She gripped the starched napkin on her lap, imagined clearing the smudge away. The red cracks staining the glass, her puckered lip print stamped, mocking her.

The Auditorium

The presentation has already begun. Mary and Ron wedge their way across a middle row in the middle school's auditorium *excuse us, pardon, thank you, sorry,* as the other couples (and perhaps some of the school's teachers?) shift their legs to make room. They hold onto the seatbacks, hunching their shoulders, trying not to obstruct the view.

The auditorium is nearly full. Paper programs flutter in hands, fanning faces beneath the kick and rise of the school's heat. They settle in wobbly seats, Ron unzipping his coat, Mary tucking her purse in the darkness beneath.

A banner hangs crooked above the stage, wavering from an unseen vent. Painted red, green, and blue lettering spells out *Central Students R The Future.* A caged wall clock's hands are stuck at two fifteen, though it is just past eight p.m. on Friday night. It is the first time the Simon's have attended one of these community presentations. Tonight's is something to do with wildlife, Mary can't quite remember. It was Ron's idea. A chance to take their mind off things. Just for an hour. One night. Mary had agreed. It was their twenty-third wedding anniversary, anyway.

The man on stage is dabbing a handkerchief to his forehead, the spotlight illuminating the sweat glistening on his face, a glare off his eyeglasses as he speaks at a podium.

"Life happens between these two fixed events," he says, "birth and death, which no species, the smallest insects nor the largest mammals prove capable of remembering."

Mary reaches behind her husband to assist him when she notices him struggling to pull his left arm free from his coat sleeve. She feels a momentary swell in her chest, happy to help, to do something with such simple purpose and effect. Ron nods back, resettling. Maybe this will be good for them, she thinks.

"How was it?" the man on stage says, with strange vibrato, mocking. "An undeniably unanswerable question for any species," he explains.

A collective laugh rises from the audience, startling Mary. What in the world is funny? She opens the paper program, scanning in the dark, for what she does not know.

"In our drive to understand the progression between these fixed points, we can turn to the Animal Kingdom." A screen lowers from the ceiling with a rattle and hum as the spotlight dims.

A close-up image of a green-eyed slimy frog appears on the screen. Murmurs sound from the crowd. Who are all these people here tonight? Mary wonders. She focuses on the frog as the man fiddles with his pointer, a red light shaking across its head.

Ron thought they ought to distract themselves. They would take a night off from visiting the hospital. Just one night. Julie would be fine. At twenty-two, their daughter was safe now. In good hands, Ron had said, reminding Mary of Lenox hospital's ranking, of the doctor's latest reassurance, of her progress so far, which was promising, her scars almost completely healed.

He is uncomfortable. Cramped between the wooden armrests, leaving no room for his wife's slender elbows which she clasps across her stomach. A hairball in his throat, he forces a swallow, then coughs instead, knocking the heel of his hand against his chest, trying to release it. The sweater Mary gifted him tonight itches at the collar and he pulls it away, the skin on his neck prickling.

Tonight was supposed to help. Tonight is for them. Tonight, they will not think of Julie, her frail frame in the cotton gown, the wilting flowers in the plastic pitcher, the nurses writing her stats on a whiteboard, while the TV plays reruns of sitcoms she doesn't laugh at. He tried to assure Mary as they drove the six familiar blocks to their middle school instead of the usual forty-five minutes to Lenox, that they would go back tomorrow. Tonight is for them. It will be interesting, he promised.

Mary averts her gaze away from the bulging frog stuck to the muddy bark of the tree. Instead, she stares at the back of the woman sitting in front of her. It dawns on her that perhaps it is one of Julie's former teachers. She has met them all, she realizes. Years of parent-teacher days, visiting open classrooms, admiring schoolwork fastened to the walls. Who is she? Maybe from third grade? Or fourth? She fastens her eyes on the back of the woman's neat black bob. It feels urgent now to recall each of her daughter's previous teachers' names. First grade, Mrs. O'Farrell. Of course, that was easy. Second grade…

A high-pitched screech blows through the microphone, jerking her attention back to the stage. Whatever is he talking about? Frogs? Death?

Grade two…she refocuses. That was Mr. Phillips. Yes. She remembers his bowties. Now, third grade…the retired nun. Ms. Kessler, Kessley, something like that. That black bob in front of her, perfectly combed, curling at the edge of her neck, she must be fourth grade, but what is her name?

A light round of applause now, but Ron has missed it. The red light draws a shaky circle on the screen, over a new image of a bullfrog. "The amphibian, literally meaning *dual life*, lives a life full of change."

Well, who doesn't? Ron thinks irritably, stretching his wool collar with his finger. Who doesn't change? He cannot get comfortable.

"They often experience two completely different realities in a single lifetime—one underwater and the other on land."

That is quite different, he supposes.

Mary decides she will say hello during intermission. Is there intermission? She checks the paper program with a flutter of panic. She needs to know if the teacher remembers Julie. She will remind her of the twelve-year-old girl who used to love lots of things, science in particular, yes, she always did very well in science, just like her father, collecting earthworms, garden bugs in dixie cups full of dirt, lining them up along her bedroom window. She was a good student. Certainly, the teacher will remember Julie.

On screen, a cluster of tadpoles swim frantically around one another, in all directions as though searching for an escape.

"Few species alter themselves as much. Change after change, adapting. However, each will spend most of its lifetime alone."

Ron has heard enough of frogs. Enough of their changes, their solitude. He shifts in his seat, bumping his wife's elbow, *sorry*, uncrosses.

It's not a bad quality, though. Important to adapt, he thinks.

Mary has a plan for intermission, but the man is droning on about spending life alone, and she wonders if she'd rather be a frog, and she tries to focus, but her mind slips away, unable to contain her thoughts as she wonders what happened between the twelve-year-old collecting bugs and the twenty-two-year-old lying alone tonight in room 413. Her face burns, and her eyes burrow into the back of the fourth-grade teacher's head, determined to think about what her name could be.

A unanimous "ooh" rises from the crowd when the picture changes to a large orangutan crouched over a mirror.

"The half-hunched position connotes an urgency here." He draws the red pointer over its rear legs. "It's clear from the tension in its legs, the muscles equally flexed. Not a relaxed position."

Ron can relate. He shifts in the seat again. He recalls sitting here for Jule's middle school graduation a decade ago. How time goes by.

"Here, the aping or mimicking behavior suggests a self-awareness," the presenter says. "The primate and mirror, a classic example."

He should take notes, Ron quickly decides with instant conviction. Julie might find some of these ideas interesting. She loves science. Or she used to anyway. He should take notes and bring them to the hospital tomorrow. He can show them to her then. They can talk about it.

He whispers to his wife, "Do you have a pen?"

"What?"

She looks at him with fright, as though she is surprised to see him sitting there beside her, as though by seeing him, she remembers that she is here, too. He does not know where she has gone to, or where she thinks she is.

He makes a writing motion with his hand.

"Ah." Mary reaches down into the dark and pulls up her purse. She feels inside, then withdraws a miniature notebook with a pen. She twists the little pen until its tip appears, then hands them over.

Maybe it was the year off from college, Mary considers. Or that apartment of hers. Anyone would feel down in that place, so dreary. The building's halls so long, crowded with other people's doors. And her last boyfriend, so...pallid is the word that comes to mind, but that's not exactly right.

Ron scratches his pen lightly on the paper.

"When a female is ready to mate, she will search for a partner and the pair will stay together only for a few days. Then they will go their separate ways."

That ex-boyfriend, Ron thinks. He wasn't a good guy. A father can sense these kinds of things. But he knows better than to place blame.

Whatever happened to Julie was about Julie. Nobody can make you… he reigns in his thoughts when he notices Mary stroking the faint blue veins along her upturned wrists.

He coughs again, more forcefully this time, and she straightens, letting go of her clasp.

It is almost time for intermission.

Some words on Sea Cows, then the speaker tells them he will resume after a short break with some fascinating views on insects.

A few clappers ignite a round of applause as a murmur grows among the crowd rising from their seats, and one by one they make their way out of the rows.

"Excuse me, hi. Hello." Mary reaches out to touch the arm of her navy blazer. She has found Julie's fourth grade teacher in the lobby.

The woman smiles, seemingly accustomed to contact with strangers in a crowded hall.

"You had my daughter," Mary explains. "Julie Simon? Many years ago. She's twenty-two now."

The woman reaches out to shake Mary's hand with a strong grip. "Nice to see you."

Just as Mary is about to say, *please remind me, I'm sorry I've forgotten, but what is your name?* Ron appears, heartily inserting himself as he wipes his chin. "Those water fountains sure aren't designed for grown-ups," he says, giving a laugh, then straightens and says, "Oh. Hello," and Mary explains, "my husband," and the teacher shakes his hand.

"Julie's teacher," Mary says, taking Ron's elbow, hoping the woman will re-introduce herself now.

"And how is she doing?" she says, distracted by someone waving at her across the lobby.

"Oh fine, good, yes," they both answer after a pause.

"I'm sorry—" she gets pulled away as another couple descends, whom she clearly recognizes. Parents of a current student, perhaps, or a recent one.

"Enjoy your evening," Ron calls, holding up a hand and turns to his wife who looks stricken.

The argyle sweater suddenly makes her very sad. She shouldn't have bought it. They'd stopped with gifts years ago. Something about it seems grotesque now.

He checks his watch. A pink prickly rash is visible around the wool collar. She wants to apologize.

"It fits you well," she concedes.

"Huh?"

"I almost got an extra large. I know you like them roomy."

"Oh! Yes," he crosses his arms across his chest. "Plenty of room. Easy to move."

She nods. "Good I got the large then," she says, her voice giving out.

Mary glances towards the auditorium doors, where a student usher is encouraging people to go back in. The presentation will resume soon.

"She wasn't very nice."

"Who? The teacher?" Ron says.

"I remember that now. She used to yell at the kids. Julie never liked that one."

"Hm."

"She could have said something. She could have introduced herself again, told us her name."

Ron shrugs.

"She didn't say anything at all. She used to yell at the kids all the time. In fourth grade. They're so young still." Her voice rises with a thin tautness that worries Ron.

The other attendees pour past them, filing back into the auditorium.

"She sees them all," Ron says with finality. Mary does not know how to respond.

She looks ill, crossing her arms over her midsection.

"You need some water? There's a fountain," Ron offers, pointing down the hall.

"No. I'm fine."

It's the dryness in her lips, the hollow under her eyes, he knows she is not fine, but it is what exists between them now, and he does know how to fix it.

"I'm gonna get some more," he tells her. "I'll meet you back in there."

"Good." She leaves as he lumbers back to the water fountain made for children.

She walks past the rows to letter K, then scoots in past the legs turning aside to make room.

In the lobby, Ron stares at the poster of upcoming events, moving his pen repeatedly around four lines of an empty box he has drawn on his pad of paper.

Back in her seat, Mary thinks how much easier it is to breathe without her husband cramped in the seat beside her. She sees the speaker in the wings, affixing the microphone onto his collar. She dreads hearing him start up again, whatever he has been talking about—tadpoles? Monkeys? She looks toward the aisle. The caged clock still shows two fifteen, but it is nearing nine o'clock. Visiting hours are until ten. They can still make it. She clutches her purse on her lap, searching the aisle for her husband. *What is he doing?*

The man walks onto the stage and welcomes them back.

"As we leave the world of animals observable with our naked eye, we move into a smaller, more private world often viewed through a lens."

Where is he?

"Insects are the most diverse, successful group in the kingdom. In this picture, we see a lion, a bird, grass, trees. But there is so much more here. There is as much life happening in this picture that we cannot see."

A collective murmur of appreciation and then Ron is back, shuffling his way into row K. Mary sits erect as he settles, despite her shaking her hand for him to wait. She grabs the armrest between them and hurriedly whispers, "I want to go."

The teacher's black bob turns slightly to the left.

"What?" he whispers back.

"We should go."

Ron checks his watch. "It's about forty minutes till the end."

"That's too late."

"It's not over yet."

"We can still make it," she whispers.

"We won't," he whispers back and then shuts his eyes, leaving Mary to gawk at his audacity.

The speaker's red pointer bounces across the screen. "The inner workings, complicated habits, patterns inherent in insect life crawling on a single leaf, for example, or between these blades of grass, or even inside the hairs on this lion."

Mary shuts her eyes, too.

"Insect life, from infancy to adulthood, progresses through many interesting stages, until an internal structure is developed."

Ron wonders if they were ants, would they go through all these stages, would they have gotten this far apart from each other? Tomorrow, he assures himself again, tomorrow they will go to the hospital. Julie will still be there. A is for Ants, he says to himself. Then he decides to catalogue a list of insects starting with the letter A. He moves on to Arachnids, keeping count.

Mary is back in room 401, watching her daughter's vacant eyes look back at her. She tucks a thin blanket around her body. *Are you cold?* she asks, and her daughter mutters something in response, but Mary cannot understand what she says. She wraps another blanket around her daughter's shoulders, moves the IV aside, glances at the numbers recording her vitals, calculating her body's functioning, her life force. *I saw your fourth-grade teacher,* she tells her. And her daughter says, *Ms. Ross?* And then Mary pops open her eyes, reaching halfway out to the black bob in front of her before pulling her hand back to her lap. That's it! Ms. Ross, she thinks, with such an enormous rush of relief, and with this breakthrough, the purpose of the night abruptly ends. They must leave. They must leave now.

Ron is halfway through B. Categorizing alphabetically in his mind the names of insects. This is something he and Julie will do together tomorrow. They will name insects, something she used to like. They will start with A and go to Z, back and forth like this. The more names he has, the longer they'll be able to play. But he is stuck on the B's. He needs one more, one more before he can move on to C. If he has a dozen names for each letter, then, he calculates, they'll have enough to play for a good amount of time. Just one more B.

But Ron is jolted by a hard nudge from his wife's elbow.

Laughter erupts from the seats around them. The screen shows a picture of two bumblebees struggling to get into one small beehive hole.

"It certainly isn't big enough for the two of them," the man says.

Mary sits forward, nudges her husband's arm again.

But Ron doesn't move; he is transfixed by the picture of the bumblebees.

Mary whispers again, "Let's please go."

Ron stares at the image, two bumblebees caught in this moment, struggling to fit their furry bodies into the single hole, as his wife pleads.

He is unable to move, his body wedged tightly in the auditorium chair. He feels on the verge of something.

Then, before turning to his wife and agreeing, before climbing from their row, quickly exiting the middle school together, and driving just above speed back to Lenox Hospital, where they have gone every night for the past two weeks, where they should be now, where their daughter will be sleeping in the dim light of the beeping room, where they will each place a soft kiss on her head before the night nurse reminds them that visiting hours are over and they can return tomorrow, he waits, right there on the cusp. Something is coming to him. He waits for it.

He stares at the bumblebees stuck in this moment that the camera has captured, that it cannot see past, that can only be explained by the man at the podium's assumption of how they managed, of what happened next, and then, finally it comes to him. And in one swift move, he shifts Beetle under Bedbug, and Butterfly to the end, and with a small rise of satisfaction at twenty-four names, he slides Bumblebee in between.

Everybody Needs Something

Thanksgiving was in a couple of months and Sal considered who he might call on the occasion he'd have his son for a holiday—Christmas or New Year's or maybe Ian's birthday, if it were to fall on Sal's allotted day, Wednesday. His parents were gone, and his ex-in-laws didn't want anything to do with Sal since the divorce, not that they'd ever wanted anything much to do with him anyway.

"You know what there needs to be?" Sal said to his friend Mark as they stretched out in opposite facing recliners inside Mark and Nadine's pawn shop. They were having an afternoon beer. One bottle of Budweiser each. Nadine, who usually worked in the store, had gone home early, and when Mark called up Sal with news of the recliners and a beer, Sal didn't hesitate to join.

"What's that?" Mark said, tapping out a cigarette from his pack. Nadine didn't want him to smoke inside, saying it stunk up the merchandise, but rarely did anyone come into the store anymore.

"There needs to be an organization," Sal said, pronouncing each of the five syllables of the word for emphasis.

"An organization, huh? What for?" Mark said, humoring him. He pulled on his cigarette.

"Like a service, someone you call up if you need some relatives for the kids. A grandparent or an uncle, you know. Someone to stand in, like borrow for the day. Easter dinner, or whatever."

"We're a pawn shop not an organization," Mark said, drawing out the final word like Sal had done.

"I know you're a pawn shop, for Christ's sake. I'm talking about borrowing, you know, like a rental." Sal cracked open the can of Budweiser.

"A rental relative," Mark said.

"That's right! Rent-a-Relative. It's got a ring to it, too." He swept his hand across the air like he was seeing the words in lights.

"Rent some relatives," Mark said, shaking his head with a single laugh.

"You'd be surprised," Sal said. "I bet a lot of folks need something like that these days." Sal crossed his outstretched legs on the recliner, fiddled with the tab on his can. "The kid's got an honor's class this year." He looked at the tiled ceiling covered with thousands of miniature holes. "That's what his mother says anyway. Three months already since I've seen him."

"Well," Mark said. "Better than three years."

Sal took a drink. The judge had threatened three years for repeated drunken offences, DUIs, causing a little ruckus at O'Donoghue's, nothing dangerous. But the lawyer got him off with probation and a license suspension. Whenever Mark brought it up, Sal went silent.

"Can't say it wasn't a good summer," Mark said.

"Yeah." Sal took a swig of beer. "It was summer."

"You're gonna be late already. It's three o'clock."

Sal jerked the recliner's footrest down and set down his empty can. Mark remained stretched out like he was sunbathing.

"Say hello to Nadine," Sal said. "And ask Jerry if he's in for cards tomorrow night. He's been out the past couple times."

"Will do." Mark reached over the recliner and stubbed out his cigarette on the wooden plank of the floor.

Sal stood with both hands planted on his hips. "You're gonna burn this place down like that."

"You in cahoots with Nadine now?"

"You don't have to be in cahoots to see burning wood makes yourself a fire. I got an honor's kid, you should listen to me." Sal tapped his finger against his temple.

"Those genes came from more than one place, you know."

Sal gave a laugh. "Yeah, whatever."

"It's three," Mark said, checking his watch again. "Go get your kid."

"You've got a hundred clocks hanging on these walls and they all say a different fucking time."

"They're for sale."

"Well, they don't work so well if you ask me."

"Three oh two," Mark said. He reached into his pocket and pulled out his car keys, then tossed them across the space. Sal caught them with one hand.

"Thanks."

Mark lifted his bottle. "Go."

Sal stopped at the door. "You know who'd use a service like that?" He didn't wait for an answer. "Petey," Sal said. "Both parents gone. His wife's, too. The kids are still young. Who'll they have for Christmas dinner? Think about it...Rent-a-Relative."

"Yeah, alright. Get a move on."

"They've got the Big Brother thing, right? Maybe Big Sister, too."

"It's the Boy Scouts you're talking about."

"I'm not talking about Boy Scouts. It's a thing—Big Brother. Like what I'm talking about here. You stand in, mentor a kid."

"You want to mentor a kid?" Mark laughed.

He was about the only person who could say something like that and laugh and not make Sal want to punch his lights out.

"No, I'm talking about when you need someone for the kid, you know, to show up, do something nice."

Mark just shook his head.

"I bet a lot of old people would want something like that."

"Yeah, grandparents whose own children don't want them—ha!"

"Ah, you don't know anything. Maybe they're somewhere else, or hell, what about the old people who never had any kids, you thought of that, wise guy?"

"It's five after. You're gonna be late."

"Why're you so bothered about being my timekeeper?"

"You asked me to tell you when it's three. Now I'm telling you it's three oh five. Buy back your goddamn watch if you want to know the time."

Sal held up his hands.

"Why don't you just call me Grandpa? You can rent me for free. Grandpa Mark."

"Ah, fuck you."

"Fuck you, too."

"Cards tomorrow then?"

"Yep. See you then."

The door dinged as it shut behind him.

Driving Mark's Buick to the middle school, Sal considered his idea and wished he were the type of person who knew how to take the leap from getting the big idea to making something of it. But he was fifty-two next month and he'd known himself for too long. He thought this was one of the overlooked benefits of being younger—the ability to think *maybe one day* about the things you knew you'd never do. No, he knew himself too well now, for better or for worse.

Mark was right; he should've left a few minutes earlier. The school bell had already rung, and the kids had been released. An enormous hive of look-alikes swarmed like bees, circling every which way, colliding, making commotion. Sal left the car across the street and stood on the far end of the field, surveying the grounds for his son.

It was his night. He got Wednesdays. That was what the judge offered, and Sal took it, no arguments. Wednesdays. It sounded like a beautiful nugget of gold. He'd treat it as such. It'd been a few years since he'd gotten to see Ian on a regular basis. This weekly Wednesdays was a new thing—Sal wanted to do it right. He would serve his probation, wait out his suspension; he would get another job soon. Larry at the garage might let him do some hourly work. Those guys were always packed over there, and Sal knew a thing or two. The case was settled, and the answer was Wednesday—a nice solid day smack dab in the middle of the week.

He'd surrendered the past three months of Wednesdays after his ex-wife planned time off from her pant-suit job to take Ian places. They were going to see her parents, the grandparents, and travel, take a family-style summer vacation, the kind Sal agreed Ian should have, though he didn't agree with the dingbat showboat of a guy she hung around with now. Sal made sure the guy knew better than to pretend he was going to be anything more than nothing to the kid.

And anyway, summer always made Sal flare a bit. And since honesty served no other purpose than to tell yourself the truth about things, he knew what he wanted to do with those summer nights—stay out late with Mark and Jerry playing cards till dawn; take his spot at O'Donoghue's Bar and drink beer with the folks he knew there; talk to a few ladies, most who wouldn't want to go home with him, except the one who always came alone and wore a leather jacket and smoked one clove cigarette after the next at her end of the bar, who insisted her name was Lizzie, though to Sal it sounded like a lie. And there was Milly, when she worked behind the bar, but that was a different story altogether being that they'd known one another for years, and it was just something they did now and then, for company. It was something they both walked away free from, neither left with any feeling other than what it was. So that was summer.

But now it was September, and the flowers were starting to fail, the branches getting bare, and there were leaves on the ground, but the weather was still hot, and it was that transitional time between the seasons when one felt big change just around the corner, when the smell and the breeze shifted just enough to announce time to start wrapping things up, time to move on. It all made Sal a little uneasy.

He was late. He walked into the center of the large field and scanned the swarm of kids scattering in all directions. Best thing to do, he thought, was just stay put. Be a landmark. Don't move. He had no idea where Ian was. All the boys looked exactly the same. He was sweating, slightly panicked. He cursed the glare from the sun making his vision warp. And then, he felt someone behind him.

"Hey," the kid said. And there was Ian, standing right there.

"Ahoy!" Sal grabbed his son, pulled him in tight. Ian's arms dangled limply by his side, and all Sal could feel in the embrace were the zippers and canvas of his backpack.

"You found me," Sal said, letting go. He blew out a deep exhale, relieved at his decision to stay put; he could navigate the storm, be captain of the ship.

"You're not hard to miss," Ian muttered at the ground. "You look like you're gonna pass out." He was fiddling with the straps on his backpack.

"It's hot," Sal said. "Come on." He started across the field.

Sal wasn't sure how to walk with his son now that he was a teenager. He wanted to grab his hand or sling an arm around his shoulders, but instead he just tried to match his gait.

"I've got Mark's car right across the street."

Ian kept his head down toward the grass.

"You kids look like you're making a break through those doors." He elbowed him lightly. "You learning something in there? I hear you've got honors." He whooped.

"I guess," he said.

"You guess, huh?"

They crossed the soggy field toward the street. Another kid called Ian's name, and Ian came to life, shouted something incomprehensible in response. His voice was different, covered with an adolescent hoarseness that Sal didn't recognize, like it was on the verge of change.

Ian's head was strained forward so far that Sal could see the vertebrae along the back of his neck. He had a pimple on his temple. His shoulders were starting to round with new muscles. He gripped the straps on his backpack as though they helped steer him.

"You got a girlfriend?" Sal said.

Ian kept his face down and picked up his pace. "Can we not talk?"

Sal nodded. "Yeah. Sure." He picked up his own pace to keep even with his son. "No more talking, I hear you. Too many people talking all the time about nonsense. We'll stop by the store. Then we'll go home. We can play cards," Sal said. They crossed the street and headed up the block past a row of cars parked along the curb. "I can teach you a couple tricks."

"I've got homework," Ian mumbled.

Everything felt out of reach. "Yeah? Alright." He yanked at his T-shirt's collar. He felt like his pores were draining buckets of lava, a stream of volcanic piss pouring over him. He hated remembering what the judge had said, worried he might be right, that he wasn't well-suited, or whatever the hell it was. Those little truths had a way of finding you, creeping their way back in, one way or another, whether you liked it or not.

All Sal wanted was a regular Wednesday with his son. And here he was feeling like his ex-wife was jerking strings, pulling Ian this way and that, refusing to look him in the eye.

"Your mom tell you to keep your mouth shut? Or maybe you're still pissed at your old man for all my bullshit?" He scanned the block, surveying the horizon.

"No," Ian muttered. "Whatever."

A father unlocking his bright red sports car gave a friendly wave like Sal was supposed to be his friend just because of their common function at school pick-up. He beeped open the doors for two bored-looking teenagers waiting on the curb. The guy looked so competent and at ease. As he started the engine and whipped out from the spot, Sal flashed his middle finger at his taillights.

"What are you doing?" Ian's voice rose to a pitch above the hoarseness. Maybe they had a chance, after all. It was good to hear his son's voice.

"You know him?" Sal asked.

"Does it matter? This is my school!" He said it with such meaning, such passion. A personality peeking through that Sal wanted to know.

The pimple on Ian's temple was red, angry looking. His eyes were wide and wet, a tint of green in the brown, like Sal's.

Sal thought of a card trick the kid would love. He'd teach it to him later, if he let him.

"You know it, kid. This *is* your school." Sal bumped Ian's shoulder. "Say it like that again. I like your conviction."

"What the fuck?" Ian muttered.

It wasn't the cursing so much as the surrendering, the petering out that irritated Sal.

"You say *fuck* now?" Sal unlocked Mark's Buick. "Your mother hear you talk like that?" Sal didn't even mean it. If anything, it gave the kid gumption. But it was the trepidation, his son retreating right there in front of him that Sal couldn't stand. He watched Ian get into the passenger seat and slide his backpack on the floor. Sal wanted to hear his voice again, what it really sounded like when he meant it, when it rose to a pitch all his own.

How was it possible to miss someone who was right in front of him? This was the sort of crap that made Sal's head hurt. The kind of crap no one prepared him for. But then again, who's ever really prepared for anything in life? That's where his ex-wife got it wrong; sure, she could plan a good party, and she never missed a beat when it came to having an umbrella or a pair of gloves. But really, who ever told her she'd marry one shithead of a fellow trying to make a decent time of things just to end up with a different, even bigger blockhead of a guy who'd keep one hand on her ass and the other on his own lousy bicep just to compare the firmer bulge. Nobody. Nobody told her. So wasn't that enough to make everyone finally just shut the fuck up and be together? You'd think. But, no.

Sal got into the driver's side and shut the door. Maybe he needed something to eat. Maybe it was the sun. Maybe he just needed to bring his son home and have their Wednesday together. He'd show him a card game or two.

"No more talking, kid, I hear you. You're onto something there."

Ian glanced at him then. A searching look, like he was about to say something.

Sal rubbed his eyes. He thought of his idea again. Maybe this Rent-a-Relative thing could go even further. If something happened to him, he could set up a good father to rent, someone waiting in the wings to take over. Why just relatives, like grandparents and aunts and uncles? Why not fathers? It could expand to whatever people might need. Mark had said it himself—people need a lot of things these days. He could scout it out, do a little research, interview applicants, check backgrounds and all that—you had to think about those things. He could build it into something big. Give his son something real, something to look forward to, something to break away towards. Something that'd be good for the both of them, if he thought about it long enough.

Ian turned his gaze back out the window.

Sal started the engine and headed the car in what he determined was the general direction toward home.

Thanksgiving Man

John and Helen had been living separate lives under the same roof for so long that when they finally got the divorce, it was less of a severing and more of a gentle coming apart like a seam whose stitch had loosened with age.

"Isn't it supposed to be harder?" Helen complained to her friend Rie while they walked through the center of their small upstate New York town. It was a week before Thanksgiving and the stores had already moved on to Christmas with their light displays in every window. Helen felt compelled to shop for gifts to bring her two grown daughters in the city on Thanksgiving.

"It's not supposed to be anything but what it is," Rie professed.

Rie did strenuous hot yoga every morning, and sometimes Helen would meet her friend outside the steamy storefront as a break from her web design work at home. An hour ago, Helen had waited outside the yoga studio in her meaningless exercise clothes that she wore mostly for comfort, while more people than she thought capable of fitting inside the store exited looking thoroughly wrung out. Helen held out a paper bag with a blueberry scone in it. "I feel like a drug dealer."

Her friend peeked inside and shook her head. "Whole30."

Helen cracked off a bite of scone for herself while they strolled the block.

"I'm just not sure what it is," Helen said. "I feel like John and I should hate each other or something. Like I should feel that deep achy depression. Like…bedridden sadness. Remember what Joanie went through with hers? She was a wreck. What's wrong with me?"

"You're guilty about feeling fine? That's *good.* We should all aspire to feel fine."

"You don't have to aspire," Helen said. "You're like…you glow or something."

"Well, second marriages are hot. What can I tell you? He wants to do it all the time. Sex does that to you."

John had agreed to give Helen the ranch house in which they'd raised both their daughters. The house was modest, and they'd had a good life in it, nothing to want to run away from; Helen had her home office set up in a way he knew she'd always loved, and he'd been sleeping on the couch so long he thought maybe it'd even be nice to have a bedroom again. Deep down he knew it was likely his fault their marriage had come apart. He knew it was written in the long line of his DNA. The way his father had never held onto a job for longer than a couple of years, John swore to himself he'd be different, that he'd be committed and loyal, and indeed he had managed to stay at the same company for almost twenty years now; however, his fated genetic failure had caught up to him in this way—his marriage. He'd even seen it coming—how Helen and he had drifted over the years, how there'd been less and less words exchanged between them, sometimes not more than a *hi* or *bye* in an entire day, how a dull grayness seemed to flatten the space around them—the piercing laugh tracks from the TV the only thing to punctuate the silence. Ever since the girls moved out, there was an emptiness that had engulfed them. Not that they fought, but still, he'd known what was happening. And he'd done nothing about it.

He moved into a one-bedroom garden-level apartment in a multi-unit building along the east side of town where the only other multi-unit buildings stretched along the narrow river. John liked the view once he stepped outside—the scatter of mid-sized boulders along the shallow river where he'd sit and look at the low hills rising in the distance—mountains he'd come to call them after all these years, though he recognized they fell short. The neighbors' footsteps traversing his ceiling rattled the single lamp on the folding table he bought from the Salvation Army, made him feel like he had company, though he'd yet to meet anyone who lived in the building.

Like countertop-stored butter—John's preferred kind to spread on toast without the force or crumble—John and Helen had slid into their official separation with an ease that felt unnatural. John wondered if maybe they had done something wrong, but the lawyer assured him it was squared away and recommended John start some new tradition, something to stake a claim on this new chapter of his life. John sat on a boulder last Saturday morning wondering what that meant. When he phoned both daughters, neither of them answered. He waited for the recorded messages to play, listened to their familiar voices, and when it prompted him to leave a message, he didn't. Helen would be with the girls in the city for Thanksgiving. She had made reservations at a restaurant in midtown with a prefixed menu. This was the first year in his life that he'd be alone for the holiday.

The number to the assisted living facility where both his parents existed had buzzed through on his phone. Every time, it shot him in the gut. At sixty-two, he knew it was rare to have both parents alive. He lowered his voice as if a deeper octave would somehow steady and ground himself for the call. Another report of decline from the director of the facility. They needed his approval for a new medication.

He arrived at the facility by noon and though they had a Christmas tree decorated in the corner of the dining hall, the hallways and living space were adorned with Thanksgiving decorations—giant cut-out cardboard Turkeys, scripted banners reading *Give Thanks,* orange and brown and yellow streamers twisted in swooping dips, Happy Thanksgiving signs covered with yellow handprints of the residents. John appreciated this accurate acknowledgement of time and date. The facility didn't rush ahead like the supermarket and big chain pharmacy stores, skipping holidays, taking for granted the easy disorientation they might cause by selling Christmas before Thanksgiving or Easter before Valentine's Day. There was an order to things, and John appreciated the facility's adherence to it.

A flyer, "Join Us for Family-Style Thanksgiving Lunch," made John pause to consider. But forearms deep in the cavity of turkeys over the past twenty-five years made him nostalgic. He loved to cook. Thanksgiving was his favorite meal of the year, he realized. If he was stranded on a deserted island and could only eat one food for the rest of his life... what kind of question was this that they'd played around the holiday table with the girls for years...what did they choose—pizza? Ice cream? Cotton candy? It was clear to him now. He'd choose Thanksgiving. That's it. Just Thanksgiving. As a general food. A combination of turkey with gravy, mashed potatoes, bread stuffing, pumpkin pie...It was one food. None of it stood alone. It only existed together. Each one needed the other.

No way, the girls would protest! Thanksgiving is not a food! But to John, right now, he determined it to be so. His new choice, his singular favorite food, the one kind he'd eat every day for the rest of his life was that combination of Thanksgiving dishes that depended on one another in order to be anything.

His chest clenched. For the first time since the divorce, a million pinpricks stung his eyes and the bridge of his nose.

He agreed to increase his parents' medications. He sat with his delicate mother and father. Kissed them on their silver heads. His parents were completely in synch. They rarely knew who John was. Their necks bore the weight of their skulls with tremendous effort. But they were still side by side, forgetting, declining, together. John left and went home to his underground apartment. He typed up a notecard-sized ad for the local newspaper. It read: *Thanksgiving Dinner Open to All. Anyone on Thanksgiving is welcome to come to 1585 Meadow Street, #1B on Thursday, November 22 at 3:00pm for a traditional Thanksgiving meal (Turkey, mashed potatoes, all the fixings…). No reservation required. No questions asked. Free.*

With the same resolve with which he and Helen together had filed for the divorce, without the obsessive, conflicted ambivalence that plagued some people he knew, John had attached his ad to the email addressed to the newspaper's classifieds and hit send.

The next day, it was printed.

Helen held the newspaper open with one hand and her phone with the other. "How do you know some crazy isn't going to show up and kill you?" she said when John answered.

Helen grew up in the city on the upper west side, and this was one of the main differences between her and John, who had spent his childhood moving from one small midwestern town to another chasing his father's sporadic employment. His family migrated on the coattails of job offers, moving to whatever factory had an opening when the current factory shed its weight or closed. John's father was weight. And as an only child, John was accustomed to being by himself. But this felt different. He didn't want to be alone for his favorite food of the year, not for Thanksgiving. He was willing to risk "some crazy" as his ex-wife put it. At least, he'd have company.

"I guess I don't," John answered.

Helen sighed.

"Well, I don't know if it's a great idea," she said.

"Maybe no one will come," John said partly to appease her, but also as a concern.

"You can come to the city, you know. With the girls and I, to the restaurant if you want."

"But what about my guests?" John said. And she knew his mind was set.

Habitual, closing *I love yous* were not a reflex. They hadn't said those words in years. Instead they said, "Well. Ok." And then they hung up without the goodbye.

For the girls, Helen picked out two small, beaded purses handmade in Nepal from Rie's favorite local store that specialized in fair trade. "You're lucky you can shop for them," Rie had said, fingering a ceramic bowl full of silver rings made in El Salvador. "I always wanted girls. I thought it'd be fun to shop with them."

"How are the boys?" Helen asked.

"Alec has a girlfriend now. Did I tell you? She's a real bitch."

Helen hushed her friend.

"What?" Rie said unphased. "She is. I hear the way she talks to him. She's always criticizing something…you're too soft, you're don't understand anything…she called him a moron the other day right there in my kitchen."

"Really?"

"At least Alec blushed. He's not oblivious. But why he stays with her, I don't know. I feel responsible."

"The girls date, but nobody that I've met. You know they didn't seem phased by the divorce?"

"If Alec marries this one, they'll definitely get divorced."

Helen bristled. She felt like her marriage's failure was somehow her fault. Who had stopped loving who first?

"First world problems," Rie said, "right?" She nodded at the picture of the young El Salvadorian woman weaving colorful straw into a basket. "Do you think they really get the profits?"

Helen said. "It says so here."

"Well, if it says so," Rie said.

"Thanksgiving presents. Is that even a thing? I don't know why I bought these purses."

"Is John still having his party?"

"Weird, right?"

"I don't know. I think it's progressive. Very inclusive."

"If he doesn't get killed," Helen said. She tucked the paper bag holding the beaded purses into her own large handbag and followed her friend out of the store.

Rie said, "You just have to enjoy the journey."

"He's not scared of crazies," Helen mused. "I never knew that."

The discount market on the outskirts of town, Evermore, had great sales and less crowds than the smaller supermarket and John loaded up his cart. Maybe it was a mistake to put *no RSVP required*. He had no idea how many people to expect, aside from his neighbor in the building next to his, Mac, who'd pushed his walker over to meet John with the folded newspaper pressed against his metal handlebars. Mac was a war veteran and never married. "This your place here?" Mac pointed a knobby finger at the ad. John introduced himself eagerly. The two men stood on the cement walk connecting their buildings as Mac told John about his life, every now and then pausing to offer up a silver flask from his coat which John declined. Mac thanked John for the invitation, said he'd be there.

John planned a meal for ten. Then on second thought, in the checkout line behind a pregnant woman unloading the mountain in her cart, he swerved his cart back into the aisles, added an extra box of stuffing, another netted bag of potatoes, and switched out his turkey for a bigger one. So, twenty. He could always freeze the leftovers.

The train to Penn Station was crowded and smelled like cigars although no one was smoking. Helen sat at a window seat and checked her texts and emails on her phone like a bad habit despite it being Thanksgiving morning. Nobody was texting or emailing her. Now that she thought about it, she questioned whether she'd ever really felt satiated. With John. Or with marriage, in general? Or life? She couldn't claim to feel more content now. She felt fine, and it was true what Rie said, everyone should aspire to feel fine. But something about that benchmark depressed Helen. Maybe she wanted to feel. "Feel" as a general state of being. Maybe it'd been a long time since she'd really just felt. Maybe "fine" was part of the problem. Maybe it'd been part of the problem all along. As the train pulled past the landscape, she looked at the smudges against the glass—signs of life—fingerprints and breath marks, sticky stains from whatever they'd been eating or drinking; she felt the lumpy indentation beneath her seat cushion—signs of all the different rears having sat where she sat now; and for the first time since the divorce, she tried to remember what it'd been like to hug John. To really hug him close. She shut her eyes and almost felt the long solid warmth of his torso, the padded wrap of his flannelled arms. But it was gone as quickly as it came.

Mac arrived first with his walker and a tall bottle of whiskey tucked under his arm. He sat on the blue velvet couch that John had found in the alley between their buildings a couple days ago. John tended to the turkey while Mac sat and drank, reading the newspaper. It was the two of them until a large woman dressed in two long sweater robes and a pair of slippers knocked gently on the open door. "Ho, ho!" John exclaimed eagerly and waved his oven mitts to invite her in. She pulled open the screen door and stepped soundlessly inside the threshold. This one Helen might've been scared of, he thought as he imagined a gun, or a handmade bomb, a Molotov cocktail, hidden inside the thick layers of her clothing, but John wasn't worried. As far as he was concerned, he had nothing to lose.

"Come in, have a seat anywhere. Enjoy the fire," John said pointing to a small faux cardboard fireplace with an unlit stack of dried logs inside. He'd found it at the Dollar Tree. The woman just stood there in the threshold, staring down at the floor. John went about his cooking. As his ad promised, he didn't ask her anything.

Just as he was ready to take the turkey out of the oven, a siren sounded outside. One slur of an alarm. John went to the door and looked outside. An ambulance was parked in front of his walkway. For a moment, John's heart skipped, and he imagined his parents inside.

The ambulance driver got out and helped an old lady from the passenger seat. The old lady held onto the driver's elbow, barely reaching up to his shoulder in height. She walked painfully slow and wore a sheer scarf tied over her white hair. Every few steps, she stopped and arched back, looking up at the driver as though to make sure he was still the one attached to her.

John pressed open the screen door.

"You the Thanksgiving man?" the ambulance driver said.

The robed woman stepped aside and into the shadows of the kitchen corner where the lamp was out. John saw her stick a square cotton oven mitt into her sweater's pocket.

Thanksgiving man. It had a nice ring to it.

"I guess I am," John said, holding open the screen as the driver guided the old lady inside and over to the velvet couch.

"First time out in years," the driver said quietly to John. "She's in the nursing home over in Ridgeview. Years," he repeated.

John looked at the old lady sitting beside Mac on the couch. She was untying her head scarf with her arthritic-looking fingers.

"Well, I'll get her back soon as we're done."

"Naw, that's alright. She paid me $100 cash for the roundtrip. I'll come back in a couple hours."

Despite John's invitation to stay, the driver had a family to get home to.

John thought of his parents and phoned the facility. He left a message for the director asking if they could transport his parents to his house. They would probably say it wasn't a good idea. This was a common theme in his life. Those closest to him telling him his ideas weren't good. Well, he'd made it this far. Maybe he'd get in the car and go pick his mother and father up himself, bring them over for the meal.

John poured a jug of wine into the mismatched glasses and set the plates around the table covered with a pumpkin adorned plastic tablecloth (on clearance at Evermore). Lastly, a young man who looked to be in his early fifties dressed in a collared shirt over a V-neck navy sweater knocked on the open door and stepped inside, awkwardly introducing himself as Jon.

"Well now there's two of us," John laughed and shook the young man's hand which was strong and warm. He set another plate at the table and despite his no questions promise, he couldn't help but wonder about this new Jon who looked like the kind of fellow who should be surrounded by a pretty wife and teenaged kids and brothers and sisters and aunts and uncles and grandparents and mothers and fathers. The kind of man who looked like he belonged to something other than himself. He looked part of something. Why was he here?

They sat around the table—John, Jon, Mac, and the old lady whose name was Doris. The robed woman stayed standing in the corner, and John set her plate on the counter. She pulled it towards her without a word.

John clinked his glass with his plastic fork. "Well. Thank you all for coming. I'm sure we're each thankful for something. So, well, we can go ahead and be thankful and bow our heads together."

Doris held her hand over her chest. "I pledge allegiance," she began with her eyes closed, "...to the flag... of The United States of America..." she continued, and after a pause, the rest of them joined in, "...and to the republic..." and when it was over, John served the food.

While everyone ate, nobody talked much aside from Mac who told stories like he was out at sea, squinting at a horizon only he could see. Stories of years past, fragmented war stories that seemed to be missing some vital components in time and space, which made them lose coherence. But it didn't matter. It added a nice background noise to the overall warm mood that fell upon the table, everyone content in their proximity to one another, no longer strangers by the very fact of the meal.

Doris was nodding off. He wondered if she knew where she was, if she realized she was in a place other than where she'd been for the past however many years. The fact moved him, that she'd come here for Thanksgiving dinner. John got up and found his checkbook. He wrote a check made out to Cash for $50 and slipped it into her purse. The cost of her ride home.

The girls were on a schedule. They both had plans to meet up with friends after dinner, so Helen would have to ride the train back right away instead of stroll down Fifth Avenue like she'd imagined them doing together. It'd only been a few months since she'd seen the girls, but they looked older, more make-up, more style. Helen slid her large handbag holding the beaded purses from Nepal under her seat. The gifts no longer seemed to match who the girls were now. Helen felt ten years behind; they'd moved on, into that glorious state of being that felt like flying once catapulted from their childhood home and into the great unknown. They were becoming. And it was happening too quickly for Helen to keep up.

The whole thing felt stilted. First of all, there was soup. Lobster bisque as an option. Or some kind of miso-based broth. Both of which felt wrong to Helen. The servers walking around with ironed aprons and platters of appetizers that were too fancy and too far-fetched a twist—gnocchi with squash and shrimp with cranberries. The girls chose for their entrées, the grilled salmon over the traditional roasted turkey, which bothered Helen, and the fancy sides (corn hash, mushroom risotto, creamed kale) were an extreme evolution from John's mashed potatoes and bread stuffing. When it came to dessert, the buffet held all kinds of decadent spin-offs and fondues, everything except the pumpkin pie with marshmallow topping that they'd eaten every year for the past twenty-five that Helen suddenly craved. She never knew how much she liked it until now. The girls were texting on their phones, making plans, and Helen unwrapped a Tums from her wallet. She wondered what the restaurant would do with the extraordinary amounts of leftovers. Such waste, she thought and when her daughters finally looked up from their phones, she asked them if they were sure they didn't want to get some more dessert before they left. But they'd barely touched what they had taken, and they were ready to go. Helen resisted the urge to ask the server for another cup of coffee and instead took the bill. When the girls asked about their father, Helen casually said he was having some friends over.

The meal was over, and it had been everything John remembered, the taste of tradition lingering in his pallet as he surveyed the remains on the table, and yet something about each dish tasted flat, like the flavors were off a half-note. Maybe it needed more salt. He thought of Helen and missed her for the first time since the divorce in a way that felt like something to recognize, though he wasn't sure what more to make of it.

Afterward, the young guest, Jon unzipped his backpack and pulled out a pink and yellow patterned apron. He put it over his head and tied it around his back. The apron only came to his hips. He ran the kitchen sink to start the dishes.

"OK, then," John nodded and stood up to help. He liked a man who helped out. They'd tackle this together.

Doris was asleep at the table. Mac was asleep on the velvet couch. The robed woman was still standing in the corner and a deep, beautiful, low humming was coming from her, the sound of an unfamiliar tune.

John and Jon stood elbow to elbow at the sink. "I'll dry," John said.

The young man washed clumsily. Unaccustomed. The apron was worn. Too small for him. It had understandably belonged to someone else.

John took the plates one at a time, dripping with suds from Jon and rubbed a dishtowel over them, stacking them face down on the counter. Each time right before Jon reached into the suds-filled sink, he patted his open palms gently against the apron pockets at his hips as though to make sure it was still there. The gesture didn't go unnoticed by John. The man kept his face down, the V-neck sweater sleeves pushed up past his elbows, his young, muscled arms working to scrub. Something about the apron squeezed John in the throat. He knew. It was obvious. There'd been a wife. Grief dripped like suds off each plate that the man handed over. It made John think of the kind of loss that changed the meaning of whatever was left behind, the kind of loss that belonged to things that at one time existed only because of something else. It was gravy without the turkey. Whoever ate cranberry sauce by itself? John didn't know that kind of loss. It pained him to think about.

The facility called on his cell and John jumped at the ring. As predicted, the director who was calling from her own home on Thanksgiving, the sounds of life filling the phone's background, said it wasn't a good idea. His parents needed to stay put. Moving them would create an unnecessary disturbance. John hung up and decided he'd bring over leftovers tomorrow. He'd sit and serve his parents the Thanksgiving food, the turkey and gravy and cranberries and mashed potatoes and stuffing all together on one plate for them to eat.

John returned to the sink, took another dripping plate and dried with the dishtowel slung over his shoulder. Beside him, Jon was crying. It was a quiet, private cry, and John didn't say a word. Who was he to disturb him with feeble consolation? The young man cried and washed and plunged his hands deep into the soap-filled sink, searching for last remaining forks and knives, and John dried, making a point to do it slowly, one prong at a time. Nobody seemed to want to rush out of there, and he didn't want to make anyone go somewhere they didn't have to be. The woman's humming made a velvety softness float throughout the space. A rumbling snore sounded from the couch. The two men stood silently side by side, carefully doing the dishes together. John beside the ghost of a woman he'd never known while the man beside him wore her empty apron.

The train home was vacant. Helen chose a seat in the middle of the empty car and sat beside the window. Her reflection in the dark glass her only company. She took out her phone and sent a text to Rie: *Happy Thanksgiving!* with a turkey emoji, and when she hit send, the text somehow went through with a burst of fireworks and balloons.

Her friend wrote back, *You OK?*

Helen nodded to herself and wiped away the first tears she'd cried in as many years as she could remember. She watched the three gray dots and then came a photo of Rie's two grown boys sitting at the dining room table covered with the festive remains of the meal. Helen looked closer and noticed someone in the background reflected in the mirror. It was Rie's second husband glancing towards the camera, presumably at Rie taking the photo. The red glare in his eyes made him look like a werewolf. Helen couldn't help thinking of what Rie had said about him wanting sex all the time. There was something predatory in his reflection, some hunger, like despite the carcass amidst mounds of food leftover on the table, he was still starving, like he wanted to eat her.

Helen thought of John in his basement apartment and could picture him vividly at the stove, preparing the turkey as he'd done for the past twenty-five years, mashing potatoes, cooking pie. He loved Thanksgiving dinner. The one night a year Helen saw him light up with such fervor. But never did she see him like that, with the red in his eyes, starving to eat her. Maybe they'd never been close enough to ever be hungry for one another. Or maybe, it was opposite, maybe they'd been so close all along that they never had to starve.

A panic fluttered in her chest, and she sat upright. She texted her daughters jointly. *Happy Thanksgiving!* she wrote again, this time without the emoji and careful not to send fireworks or balloons. Within seconds, two separate texts popped up. One, a thumbs-up emoji. The other, *thx.* She texted each back the kissing face emoji, hearts flying in the air. Nothing came in return.

Then she sent a text to John. Simple, straightforward, courteous, *Happy Thanksgiving.* Something to acknowledge the two-and-a-half decades they'd eaten Thanksgiving dinner together, no hard feelings, things change, life goes on. And yet as soon as she pressed send, she felt an uncomfortable eagerness, staring at the screen, waiting for a response to come through, while the invisible particles of her words decoded, soared through space via mysterious cellular networks, translated into some encrypted cyber system and fed to network towers before being intercepted and reinterpreted, the message eventually materializing on their separate devices, connecting them.

Acknowledgments

I am so grateful for the support in receiving this award. Thank you to Columbus State University, CSU Press, University of Georgia Press, DLJ Books, Allen Gee, and the late Donald L. Jordan for the generosity and encouragement of the Donald L. Jordan Prize for Literary Excellence and making this book possible. Thank you to Debra Jo Immergut for choosing my work, I am honored.

Thank you to the editors at the following literary magazines for their belief in the work and who first published some of these stories: *Swamp Pink, Vestal Review, Connotation Press, Adelaide Literary Magazine, Story South, Blackbird, Fifth Wednesday Journal.* These stories were written over many years, and I have been lucky to work with numerous teachers along the way, a few who made a specific impact—Jonathan Dee, Jhumpa Lahiri, Beth Nugent, Richard Bausch, the late Kevin McIlvoy, the late Ed Dorn, and my earliest mentor, the late Lucia Berlin. Gratitude to the community at Key West Literary Seminars and for the generous support of their Emerging Writers Awards and to Monson Arts for the Writer-in-Residency.

Thank you to my writing friends and literary communities offering vital support over the years. Sara Lippmann, Michael Zapata, Heather Dewar, Rebecca Leece, Rachel León, Lara Henneman, Vesna Jaksic Lowe, Kristin Vuković, Nishanth Injam, Christine Vines, Jenny Halper, Shayne Terry, Ethan Rutherford, Dan Pope, Milda De Voe's Pen Parentis Accountability Group, Louise Marburg and her story book club, Diane Zinna and her grief writing offerings, The New School MFA program, Bread Loaf and Sewanee Writing Conferences, and my writing group for feedback on many of these stories—Aimee LaBrie, Erin Striff, and Yelizaveta Renfro. I'm also grateful to Sara, Mike and Debra for taking time to read and blurb my debut—it means so much.

I'm thankful for longtime friends, Bridgette Buckley Bertran, Diane Van Horn (in memory), Kelly Siske Dunworth, Jen Rose, and my CT communities, including Sara Huber, Jen Allen, Sarah Fite, Lauren Krasnow, Jodie Sadowsky, Allison Freeman, Jordi Hertz, Ellery Smith, Susan Mazer, and the organizations I've been lucky to be involved with that work hard to create social impact through the arts, including Charter Oak Cultural Center, CT Center for Nonviolence, CT Office of the Arts, Hartford Performs, Narrative 4, The Pollination Project Greenhouse, National Arts Strategies Community Fellows, including my recent PEG cohort, who help me integrate my Poetry on the Streets work with my writing work.

To my family members for always being there and cheering me on. Hershy Pappadis, Thomas Pappadis (in memory); my sister Stephanie Corrado and family; James Pappadis; Arnold Faranello (in memory); and Stefanie Zizzo.

And to my husband, Scott, for being my best of everything, for the love, encouragement, and belief, and without whom none of this would exist. And to my boys, Tate and Sage. You guys are the world to me. I am so lucky to have you.

About the Author

Melanie Faranello's stories and essays have appeared in numerous publications, including *Swamp Pink*, *Electric Literature*, *StoryQuarterly*, *Hippocampus*, *Vol 1. Brooklyn*, *HuffPost Personal*, *Blackbird*, *StorySouth*, *Catamaran*, *Connotation Press*, and elsewhere. A two-time Pushcart Prize nominee, recipient of a Writer-in-Residence Award from Monson Arts, and an Artist Fellowship from CT Office of the Arts, she won Key West Literary Seminars' Emerging Writer Award for Novel-in-Progress. She holds an M.F.A in Creative Writing from The New School. She is also the founder of Poetry on the Streets, a community engagement project. Originally from Chicago, she lives with her family in West Hartford, CT and is at work on a novel. Read more at www.melaniefaranello.com

The Donald L. Jordan Endowment was established in 2016, in part, to facilitate the formation of Columbus State University Press, which was officially formed in 2021. CSU Press is pleased to recognize Mr. Jordan as the founder of the press, which serves as the publishing venue for the Donald L. Jordan Prize for Literary Excellence, and for The Nature Series at DLJ Books. DLJ Books has been installed as a permanent imprint at the press. Mr. Jordan's foresight made CSU Press a reality, and we are grateful for his generosity. Mr. Jordan passed away on May 15, 2023 after a very successful business career. The author of literary novels, short stories, and works of non-fiction, he was also particularly interested in helping other writers attain publication.